Best wish
Margaret

About the Author

Margaret Moore was born in the East End of London during the war years. Leaving school at the age of fifteen with no qualifications, she took further education to achieve the skills of a secretary. During this career, spanning thirty-seven years, she worked as a legal secretary in London, Essex and Suffolk, retiring in 2007. She began her writing career with a children's book. She lives in Suffolk with husband, Norman. They have two sons, two grandsons and a great granddaughter.

Chances Taken

Margaret Moore

Chances Taken

Olympia Publishers
London

www.olympiapublishers.com
OLYMPIA PAPERBACK EDITION

A CIP catalogue record for this title is
available from the British Library.

ISBN: 978-1-78830-384-2

This is a work of fiction.
Names, characters, places and incidents originate from the writer's
imagination. Any resemblance to actual persons, living or dead, is
purely coincidental.

First Published in 2019

Olympia Publishers
60 Cannon Street
London
EC4N 6NP
Printed in Great Britain

Dedication

For my brother-in-law, James Blanchard, who knew many characters in London's East End and enjoyed their stories.

CHAPTER ONE

The noise. The shouting. It was becoming unbearable. The atmosphere in the kitchen was more than they could bear.

Beryl was standing in the doorway with two bags packed and bulging fit to bust. Her mother, Mavis, and gran were both sitting at the table which was the only obstacle keeping them apart from this child who thought she was already a woman. At seventeen, she was far from that.

The make-up which she now used and thought propelled her into the starlet arena, only made her look like a child hiding behind a mask. Beryl had the confidence of youth and the dreams of a generation that was not going to be kept close to home. This was 1953 and it was time her mother and gran realized she knew what she wanted out of this new post-war life.

The magazines she had secretly been reading were full of American film stars and their way of life. Music, make-up and fashion were what her new life would become, even though it would mean trying to get a better paid job instead of the one she had at the local Woolworth store. There had to be a job somewhere she could get which would make people notice her and, hopefully, get her photo into one of those magazines.

She would need to buy clothes which would show off her figure, which she had been told by one of the cheeky blokes she worked with, was worth showing off.

Once the shouting subsided on all sides, Beryl stared directly at her mother.

"When I walk out of this house, my name will not be Beryl. It's one of the worst names I can think of. My new name is going to be Donna."

The look on Mavis's face was of disbelief. What was happening? She clenched her fists, her nails digging into the palms of her hands.

"What are you talking about? Don't be stupid. Where's that come from?"

Mavis and Granny Flo, of course, had no idea that Beryl and her best friend, Ann, had been making a list of all the starlets' names in their favourite magazine and had decided Donna sounded 'with it' which was the phrase to use now.

Living in sin. That's what Flo had called it. She didn't hold with it.

Beryl's boyfriend, and she couldn't bear to speak his name, might have got the chance to rent a couple of rooms in a friend's house so they could be together but, it wasn't right. If her Jack had been alive, he would have put a stop to it.

What's more, the boyfriend had arrived on the scene in such a secret way that everyone in the Taylor household had wondered if he was on the run from someone or something.

Apparently, Beryl had been seeing Tom for about two months. Even that wasn't gospel.

At seventeen she was very willful.

Flo had been widowed at the end of the First World War. She had eventually moved in with her daughter, Mavis, and son-in-law. As their family came along, she had been a great help to her daughter, looking after their children while Mavis went to work at the local gas mask factory as her husband had been drafted into the army.

With history repeating itself, in 1944 Mavis had received the dreaded news that her husband had been killed in action.

With Beryl eight years old and little George only six, it would be a struggle to survive but, at least she had the support of everyone around her in this street, many of them in the same situation as she was.

'This street' as she called it, was Francis Road.

All the streets around this part of east London had been named after saints, though God knows why. There were a lot of Chinese and Italians living here, some of them second generation. Surrounded by Peter Parade, where the most shops were, Christopher Lane, which was a cut through for the kids to get to school, St David's Road, St Mary's Road and St Paul's Road. With all this Christianity in their midst it was still a struggle for the local vicar to entice people into the usually half empty church which stood lonely and decaying. Flo's Jack had said the only use it was put to was for births, marriages and deaths and all of those you had to pay for despite the wealth that was in most church coffers. He used to go on for hours about the church robbing the poor every time repairs were needed. Flo was convinced he'd go to hell when his time came. Perhaps that's where he ended up.

Flo heaved her ample body up from the kitchen chair. She was a big woman, which hadn't been altered over the years despite all the food rationing. Her size made her seem formidable.

The whole street knew her as Granny Flo and she was the one to run to when there was a problem. She was, though, never judge nor jury. She was always fair and so when Beryl started getting ideas about moving out, she tried to reason with her and asked if she knew what she was getting herself into.

"Is this bloke expecting you to help pay the rent? Is he expecting you to get back to your rooms every day after work and cook a dinner? Is he going to want ...?"

Before she could say any more, Beryl stepped forward.

"Stop it. I know what you're doing. You think I haven't thought about all that. If you knew what Tom was like, you'd know he will share all those things. I just know he will."

Flo had hardly moved from where she was standing. She pursed her lips and, looking down, her many chins seemed to collide with each other.

"Are you telling us that you've talked all this over with this bloke? Because, if you are saying that, I don't believe you. The only thing he wants is to find someone who'll keep house for him, provide for his comforts and let him have his way with you. If that's what your life with him amounts to, God help you."

Mavis continued to sit silently at the table. Flo continued on. She had a lot more to say. Her face was becoming flush now.

Staring directly into Beryl's face, she said, "Do you know what the worst thing about all this is? It's the neighbours and everyone else knowing about it. They'll be talking about it behind our backs. They will be thinking of you as a slut. They will find out all right."

Before any more could be said, Beryl moved forward and leaned across the table. Her auburn hair which had always been gently held back by a ribbon, now fell loosely onto her shoulders and partly masked her face. It was, she thought, the look of a starlet.

Looking at both of them, the worst possible words were blurted out.

"I don't care what the neighbours think. My life is nothing to do with them."

Mavis, who had been waiting for this nightmare to end, suddenly woke up.

"Beryl," she shouted.

"Stop this now before it's too late. You don't know what it's like living with a man. You were too young to really know your dad when he died. You think you know this Tom but wait until he's had a few drinks with his friends. They will want to know what you are like and how far you will go. What do you think will happen if you get pregnant?"

Suddenly, you could hear a pin drop in the silence.

Beryl straightened up.

"Pregnant! Of course I'm not going to get pregnant. Tom knows how to avoid all that."

Flo slumped back onto her chair.

Looking up to the ceiling, she said, "God help us all. I thought the worst was over when the war ended, but this, I can't see a way out of it."

At that point the front door opened and then slammed shut. George was home. At fifteen he had left school and got himself a job in the local bakers. He was learning a trade and enjoying it.

As soon as he walked down the passage and into the kitchen, he stopped dead in the doorway. His mum and gran were sitting at the table like statues, perfectly still and silent.

Beryl was bending down to grasp the handles of her bags. She stood up.

"Out of my way, George. I'm going."

He stepped aside.

"So, you've told them then."

She flounced past him and made her way to the front door. She turned and took one last look behind her, opened the door and went out, slamming it shut in a final fit of defiance.

Mavis and Flo were staring into space. Their expressions were of shock and defeat.

The first one to recover was Mavis. Flying into a rage, she shouted at George.

"Do you mean to tell me that you knew all this was going on and you didn't say anything. I can't believe you thought it was all right. It's not the way you were brought up."

Before she could continue, George strode across the kitchen heading for the scullery. He was after a drink.

Flo blocked his path.

"Oh, no, you don't. You can get a drink when you've told us what's been going on."

He sighed, his shoulders sinking.

"Beryl swore me to secrecy and so I kept quiet. She's been planning this for weeks. When Tom said he'd found a place they could live in, she was over the moon. She knew you'd be annoyed."

"Annoyed. I'm more than annoyed," screamed Mavis.

George had never seen his mum so angry. It was worse than when he'd taken some money from her purse to buy sweets.

Mavis stormed on.

"Who else knew about it? I haven't heard any rumours and I can't believe Nel at No. 5 doesn't know."

George leaned against the wall in the doorway. He felt almost relieved that the secret was out now. He couldn't understand why Beryl wanted to move out. Home was all right and, now that he had a job, he had money to spend on whatever he wanted. Beryl was going to have to share her wages with Tom. In his naïve way, it seemed no different than having to give up some money for her keep as she was doing now. It hadn't occurred to him that the conditions she would have to meet for her freedom would be life changing.

After such a traumatic parting, the room suddenly seemed to close in on Flo. She silently went into the front room and gazed through the net curtains onto the street. As she tried to focus on both her view and her thoughts, she found it was almost impossible.

The rest of the day passed with not a mention of Beryl. Even when Mavis laid the table for their tea, she made no reference to Beryl. She simply served up the sausages and mash giving George an extra portion which he devoured with relish, secretly pleased that it might now mean every mealtime he was going to get more on his plate because there was extra to go around.

The next morning it was raining. It was still dark outside because low cloud hung over the street like a shroud covering a body. Mavis looked at the bedside clock for the umpteenth time and the hands hadn't moved much. It was still only 6 o'clock.

The curtains in the cramped bedroom were closed. She shared the room with her mother. The dreary brown floral wallpaper had been put up years ago when it had been the most popular pattern. The paint on the back of the bedroom door had been wiped down so many times over the years when her mother had decided to have a spring clean that it now was almost as thin as an egg shell.

There was just enough room for the two single beds and a cupboard to hang their clothes. It wasn't a wardrobe, there had been no room for one, just a tall cupboard.

They were both fed up with this rabbit hutch existence but there had been no alternative. Beryl needed her own bedroom when she became a teenager and George certainly didn't want his mates to know that he was sharing a room with his sister. The only private place for this family was the shed in the garden which housed the toilet.

In the stillness of the room, the only sound was Flo's heavy breathing and the occasional snore. She had been able to sleep through the air raids when they started and had to be woken up to get to the shelter. Mavis, who had been awake most of the night, wondered how she did it.

The click and squeak of George's bedroom door opening broke her silent thoughts. He had to be at work by 6.30. Luckily, the baker he worked for was only a few minutes' walk from the street. There would come a time when he would have to be there much earlier but, at the moment he was only a trainee. The baker was still deciding if he would be the person for the job.

Mavis rose from the bed in a much practised way so that she didn't disturb her mother and reached for her dressing gown. As her arm stretched out, her elbow knocked against the clock which was balanced precariously on a small stool between the beds and it fell onto the floor, the thin covering of lino echoing the sound. Flo woke with a start.

"What's happening?"

"Sorry, Mum. I was trying to be clever and not make any noise, but you know what it's like, the more careful you go, the more noise you make."

Downstairs in the kitchen the kettle was already on and the bread board and knife were in the centre of the table. George had busied himself and then got ready for work. As Mavis walked over to the dresser, everything seemed normal. Taking the mugs over to the table she automatically placed them next to the teapot which was waiting to be warmed and made ready for the first brew of the day. This day, though, was going to be far from normal.

Beyond the front door, the properties in Francis Road were like little fortresses. They were built of red brick by Victorian workmen who had taken a pride in their work. They had survived two world wars and many other human conflicts. They stood like sentries, their rustic colour topped by dark slate roofs.

The tenants were a mixed bunch. Many of them had found accommodation here over the years whenever a property became vacant if someone died or if a parent needed to be looked after and family took up residence to care for them.

Their landlords were varied and not all of them were reasonable and fair. Some of the properties were in need of repairs but most of the tenants kept quiet in case their complaints drew the attention of the landlords who they knew wanted to get the council to rehouse the people in this street. A landlord could sell the properties to the council who, in turn, were looking to demolish them and use the area for industry.

There were many new towns springing up on the outskirts of London which needed people to bring them to life.

When Len returned home after 1918, he had lost a leg and was never the same character he had been. He lived in the house on the corner of the street with his wife, Edna. She never stopped telling people that he had lost his leg but not his way home. The joke was that, in his time, he was quite a drinker and could always be seen staggering home from the pub, never losing his way. Even when he had to use a crutch to keep himself upright, he rarely fell over. The street knew him as One-leg Len.

Further along was shifty Sam and his brother, Colin. They had moved in when their mother died. They had a removal business which consisted of one lorry and a couple of sack barrows. If it wasn't nailed down, they would shift it for you.

Annie and Fred were a bit further along the street. They had five children and, most of the time, at least one of them was in trouble. Annie did her best to keep order, but it was difficult. Fred who worked at the docks never seemed to be home. The local bobby, Doug, was seen visiting their house more than Fred, trying to get the boys sorted out.

When the government announced on 1st September 1939 that all young children were to be evacuated from London, Annie had mixed feelings. She finally agreed to let three of the kids go, but insisted her youngest two should stay. Her two boys, John and Harry, and daughter, Sarah, were sent to families in Kent. It was the making of them. The boys soon settled into life in the country and were billeted with a couple who were amazed at their survival skills and thought it was because they had grown up in London. They weren't too keen on the village school though because it was difficult to bunk off lessons. The teacher soon became an expert on tracking them down.

Sarah was taken in by a farmer and his wife. They treated her as their own and were secretly thrilled to look after her, having lost their own daughter who had died from whooping cough during an epidemic which also took some of the other village children.

Flo was amazed when the boys returned home in 1944. They were now 12 and 14 and too much trouble for the Kent couple to deal with. She had spent many hours with Annie, helping her cope with them.

Sarah had said she wanted to stay with the Kent family. During those four years away, she had become quite the little lady and preferred it to home. Sarah didn't want to come back to her previous life. That had been another episode when Flo had given advice to Annie.

Flo made her way downstairs, her heavy tread only slightly muffled by the thin runner. Mavis looked at her as she almost stumbled into the kitchen, still weary from the day before. She was worried about her mother. She was too old to be bothered with all this trouble with Beryl.

Pouring the tea, Mavis said, "I might go into Woolworths today to see if I can get a chance to speak to Beryl in her lunch hour. You never know, she might already be having second thoughts."

Flo almost smiled.

"I think it's far too early for that. I'll give it a week."

The laughter they could suddenly hear through the thin

walls of next door where Nel lived was almost a prophesy, although Mavis and Flo didn't know what she was laughing at. It was as if she already knew that Beryl had moved out and Nel was enjoying the situation.

Flo stood up and started hacking away at the bread. She meant to slice it but, in her anger, she was destroying it.

"Mum, calm down. You're getting yourself all worked up."

Mavis was thankful that George had already left for work. She didn't want him to see his gran in such a state.

Flo wasn't ready to calm down.

"What do we know about this bloke Beryl's shacked up with? Where's he from? What does he do for work? How old is he?"

The questions kept tumbling out.

She was getting short of breath. The bread knife in her hand was being pointed in thin air every time she came up with a question. Mavis was now getting really worried.

Before she could think what to do next, there was a tap on the glass panel in the front door which was quickly followed by the clatter of the letter box opening.

The familiar tones of Nel could be heard as she called out.

"I could hear the tea cups clattering so I knew you were up and about. Can I come in for a minute?"

Flo looked at Mavis.

"What the hell does she want this time of the day? It's as though she can smell trouble. You'd better let her in."

Flo was still standing at the table, the bread knife in her hand. She looked menacing.

As Nel came into the kitchen she stopped very abruptly,

looking at Flo.

"That's the reason I'm here," she said, pointing to the knife.

Her hand had a tea towel wrapped around it. I cut me finger quite bad and I don't have a plaster in the house. Have you got one?"

The tension in the room seemed to melt away. Mavis was thankful.

"Yes, I'm sure we have."

Going over to the dresser, she pulled a drawer open and produced a battered box of plasters.

"How big is the cut? Let's have a look at it."

Nel carefully took the tea towel away from her hand and unclenched her fist. Flo looked at it.

"That's not much of a cut and it looks as though it's stopped bleeding anyway."

Taking a plaster out of the box, she handed it to Nel.

"There you are. That'll do it. Now perhaps we can get on with our breakfast."

Nel headed towards the passage and turned in the doorway.

"I thought I saw your Beryl going out yesterday with a couple of bags. Has she gone on some sort of holiday?"

That did it. Mavis felt like hiding.

Flo casually said, "No, she's taken some bags of stuff into work for a friend."

With a huge sigh which made her shoulders drop, she said, "We'd like to get on with our breakfast now if you don't mind."

Nel got the message and left.

Going over to the cooker, Flo touched the side of the kettle. It was now lukewarm.

"The tea you poured out has got cold and the kettle's gone off the boil. I haven't had a drink yet and that cow hasn't missed a trick."

Mavis knew today would be difficult to get through but, at this moment, she didn't know how bad it would get.

Mavis glanced at the clock. It was still early, only half eight. She didn't want to go out yet because it was raining again. She looked across the room and at the scullery window. The rivers of rain followed a path and disappeared where the frame came into view. It was washing the dust away that had accumulated after a few dry days. I wish, she thought, there was some way of washing away all the problems she was now facing with Beryl.

The clink of milk bottles being left on the front step broke her train of thought. She automatically got up and made her way along the dark passage. Opening the front door, she could see Routine Rosie trudging along in the rain. She quickly picked up the bottles and ducked back in. She didn't want to get caught by Rosie or she would feel obliged to ask her in out of the rain. You could set your alarm clock by Routine Rosie. Every day she kept to the same times for leaving her house, going shopping and returning home. She would then put a chair in her doorway and sit down for a couple of hours, whatever the weather, hoping a neighbour or, even a stranger, would pass by so that she could stop them for a chat. Living alone after her husband died, and with no family, she needed to speak to somebody, anybody, and the conversation always seemed to be a repeat of the one she had had the day before.

None of the neighbours let on that they had heard it all before.

Mavis needed to go upstairs to make her bed. Once at the top of the stairs and, standing on the tiny landing, she could see into Beryl's bedroom. She instinctively wanted to go in but, somehow, she couldn't. It was a forbidden place when Beryl was here. She had made it quite clear that it was private.

Well, she thought, she's not here now.

Beryl had left the room very tidy. It almost looked as though she had prepared it for her return.

Going over to the little table by the bed, Mavis saw the silver crucifix and chain lying there. It seemed like a final act that she had left her old life behind. That crucifix had been a Christmas present when she was five years old. Mavis left it undisturbed.

She went over to the small wardrobe and opened the door. There were still clothes hanging in there. She had taken all her favourites with her. It seemed as though she'd left her options open and, if things didn't work out, she would return. Mavis smiled and left the room, quietly closing the door.

By the time she made her way along the street, the rain had stopped and it looked as though the day would brighten up. When she reached the shops, the usual group of neighbours were already queuing and, amongst them, she could see Nel. Her first thought was that Beryl leaving home with bags would give Nel a head start on the expected rumours which were bound to emerge. There was no dodging them all. She'd have to be on her guard.

"Hello, Mavis. You all right?"

It was Annie.

"I heard on the wireless this morning that food rationing

is ending next year. About bloody time too. My Fred says it's a scandal they've kept it on so long."

Before Mavis could make any comment, Edna came shuffling along. As she got nearer to them all, the usual odour, which signalled her presence, seemed to reach them first. She never seemed to change her clothes. She even went shopping in her floral wrap-around apron complete with weeks of stains down it.

Nel was the first one to break the group up.

"I've got to love you and leave you all because I want to get down the market to see if I can get some decent onions instead of those soft ones they sell at the corner shop."

"Get yourself to my Harry's stall. He only buys quality veg. He'll see you all right."

It was Annie, whose eldest was a market trader.

"Where you off to this morning, Mavis?"

It was Nel. Mavis knew Nel couldn't care less where she was going. It was the start of the fact finding she was going to launch. Mavis was prepared.

"I'm making my way up to Woolworths to see Beryl. She forgot to take her packed lunch. She'd forget her head if it wasn't screwed on. You know what these young girls are like."

Mavis was pleased with her performance and started walking off towards the high street. The shout from behind her from Nel made her heart thump. Nel drew closer.

"I was going there anyway at some time today. We could go together. I can go to the market later."

That was the worst thing she wanted to hear.

The Woolworth store was huge. The large wooden blocks of counters throughout the store were all filled with items of every description. They were all positioned in rows and seemed to go on forever. The familiar smell of the waxed and polished woodwork filled the air.

Beryl had said she was working on the counter which sold dressmaking products. There were cottons, needles, tape measures and every other item you could want for sewing. Mavis knew exactly where that counter was. She couldn't get rid of Nel though. She had hoped they would part company once they were in the shop but Nel was sticking to her like glue.

Winding their way between counters, Mavis was looking ahead but couldn't see Beryl. There was a girl she didn't know standing behind the counter straightening some of the ribbons. She looked up.

"Yes, can I help you?"

"I was hoping to see Beryl. I'm her mum."

The girl stopped tidying up.

"She didn't turn up for work this morning and so they put me on here. What's wrong with her? Have you come to see the supervisor? She's really annoyed about her not turning up. She had a day off last week."

Mavis looked surprised.

"She didn't tell me she had a day off last week."

Nel was silent but taking all this in.

"She hasn't been ill and so I really don't know what's going on. When she left home, she was fine."

The girl went to the other end of the counter to serve a customer. Looking over her shoulder she called out, "You'd better see Mrs Davenport while you're here. She wants to know what's going on."

Mavis thought so do I.

Nel finally broke her silence.

“Never you mind, dear. There’s bound to be a simple answer why she isn’t here. She couldn’t have been in an accident or you would have heard. Do you want me to come with you to see this Mrs Davenport?”

Pausing, to try to take in what she was hearing, Mavis said, “No, Nel. That’s all right. You get on with your shopping.”

A disappointed Nel said, “Are you sure?”

“Yes. I need to see this woman and I don’t know how long I’m going to be.”

CHAPTER TWO

Mrs Davenport turned out to be everything Mavis thought she would be. Very businesslike. Prim and looked like a school headmistress.

She ushered Mavis into a small room on the floor above the shop.

The room had two grey metal filing cabinets along one wall and there was a wooden desk in front of them. A black telephone stood in pride of place on one corner of the desk and a shallow wooden box was positioned on the other corner. There were some pencils and a black fountain pen lying by the phone with some notepaper. The small window in front of her didn't give much light to the sterile room because the next building to Woolworths was only about two feet away. Mavis felt trapped.

Pointing to the chair, Mrs Davenport said, "Do sit down, Mrs Taylor."

Mrs Davenport pulled her chair away from the desk and sat down. Mavis sat on the other chair which had been placed dead centre from Mrs Davenport. She felt like she was the woman's target.

"Now, do tell me why Beryl didn't come to work today."

The room fell silent.

"I don't know. She hasn't been ill, and she didn't say anything about missing work. I can't think what's got into her."

Mrs Davenport got up and went over to the first filing cabinet. Pulling one of the drawers out, she produced a brown paper file and put it on the desk.

The noise of the drawer clattering shut seemed to echo around the room. She sat down.

Before opening the folder up, she said,

"There have been one or two days that she has taken off but, in the past, she has always booked them off."

She looked directly at Mavis, waiting for a response.

Mavis drew in a deep breath.

"I can't give you an answer at the moment, but I intend to find out what she's up to. Is her job still here for her?"

Mrs Davenport leaned back in her chair.

"If she can be relied on in the future, yes she still has a job. She is a popular member of staff and we would not want to lose her. Just let me know, as soon as possible, what's going on."

They then parted company.

On the way home Mavis suddenly realized she didn't even know where Beryl was now living. This was a nightmare and it was getting worse as the day went on.

When she got back, Flo was in the garden putting the dripping washing on the line. There she stood, basket of washing at her feet, pegs fixed firmly between her lips.

Hearing the front door close, she looked over to the scullery. Mavis emerged.

She put her bag down and said, "I need a strong cup of tea. I don't know yet how I'm going to deal with this. Nel came to Woolworths this morning with me. I couldn't get rid of her.

Her imagination is going to be in full swing now because Beryl didn't turn up for work this morning and she saw I was surprised at that."

Flo took the pegs out of her mouth.

"What's going to happen if she loses her job? If she can't help out with the rent, that bloke of hers will soon turf her out."

Mavis leaned against the back door.

"I realized walking home, I don't even know where she's living. How am I going to find out?"

Still standing in the garden beneath the dripping washing, Flo said, "It's that friend of hers you need to speak to. What's her name, Ann. She will probably know. They are as thick as thieves, those two.

That brought a smile to Mavis's face.

"Yes, I forgot about her. I'll go and see her later. I know where her mum lives."

Mavis knew the girl's mother worked in Benny's Café along the high road. She didn't want to wait until evening before she went round to see her and so decided to pay her a visit at Benny's. She wasn't sure if she ought to do this. It was all something new to have to deal with. She wanted to get this sorted out. Her nerves were now beginning to come to the surface. She had an awful sick feeling in the pit of her stomach and she realized her fists were clenched in the same way they had been when she was talking to Mrs Davenport.

"I'm going round to see Ann's mum this morning. I can't wait for her to get home from work. I've got to get something sorted out so I can get back to that supervisor woman. Honest, mum, if you had been there this morning. I felt like I was the one in trouble."

"It's the girl you want to speak to. Not her mum. She might not want to tell you what's been going on if her mum is there."

Mavis frowned.

"You're right. I never thought of that. I got meself all fired up to speak to her mum when, as you say, it's the girl I need to get in touch with. I wonder where she works."

Picking up the empty laundry basket, Flo made her way indoors, leaving the unused pegs clamped along the washing line looking like fallen soldiers.

"Let's get the kettle on. I'll be able to think better when I've had a drink. I might do us a sandwich as well. There's some corned beef in the cupboard. I don't know where the morning's gone."

Just as they sat down, there was a knock on the front door.

"I don't believe this. How do people know when you're just about to eat? We haven't got a sign outside, have we, saying food is being served?"

Flo was getting tetchy.

"I'll go." Mavis could see who it was knocking because Annie's familiar shape was showing through the glass panel. She opened the door.

"Hello, dear. I've just come from the market and you'll never guess who I saw. It was your Beryl and it's a weekday. I thought to meself, that's unusual. She had some bloke with her and I didn't recognize him. I was going to say hello, but she saw me and the two of them went in the other direction."

Mavis opened the door a bit more.

"You'd better come in. We were about to have a cup of tea anyway."

"Oh, I don't want to disturb you. I've got me own stuff to do, but I thought I'd better let you know about Beryl. I hope she's all right."

Mavis smiled.

"Thanks for letting me know. I'll speak to her when I see her later."

Flo, sitting in the kitchen, had heard the conversation.

"I bet Nel has been talking and it was to Annie. I don't suppose Annie would have thought anything about seeing Beryl in the market if Nel hadn't mentioned your visit to Woolworths. I bet she's added her own version of things to it as well."

Sitting down to have her sandwich and tea, Mavis said, "Who's going to know where Ann works?"

She wondered what George knew. He'd probably have some idea.

She was like a cat on hot bricks all afternoon waiting for George to finish his shift at the bakers and get home. Would he tell her if he knew or, had he promised not to let on about the girls and any plans they'd made.

As soon as he came into the kitchen, he knew something was up. His mum and gran looked like they were sitting almost positioned to pounce on him. He guessed it would be about Beryl. What had she done? She had really dropped him in it.

"Honest, Mum. I don't know where she's living. She wouldn't tell me because she knew you'd want to know."

George was feeling very defensive. He didn't know it would be like this after Beryl left. His mum and gran had been firing questions at him since he came in and that was ten minutes ago.

"All she told me was that Tom has a friend who's a photographer and he asked Tom to look out for pretty girls that he could use as models. He was going to take their pictures and try to get magazines to buy them. It was Tom's job to put the girls in touch with him. He's paying them some money if they agreed."

Flo put her hand up to her mouth. She drew in a deep breath.

Seeing his gran's reaction, he was getting scared.

"What's wrong with having your picture taken? He can take mine if he's going to pay for it."

Flo was trying not to alarm him but was trying to think of a way to find more out about this bloke.

"Let me do you a sandwich and a drink."

Slicing the bread, she was trying to stay calm.

"Beryl didn't go to work today. She was in the market though because Annie saw her. She was shopping with her boyfriend. Annie said she didn't know him though."

George was patiently waiting for his sandwich and didn't offer any more information. It was unusual, he thought, that she would do him a sandwich at this time of the day.

With the sandwich in front of him, she knew she wouldn't be able to get any sensible answers out of him. He obviously had no idea of the danger his sister could be in.

Mavis came into the kitchen and started tidying things on the dresser which really didn't need tidying.

Trying to sound casual, she said, "You know Beryl's friend, Ann. Do you know where she works? They used to meet up sometimes and have their sandwiches in the park. I wonder if they'll still do that."

With a mouthful of bread and cheese, George almost literally spat out, “I suppose so. She only works at that place that makes curtains. The one round the back of the library.”

Mavis smiled. At last she had something to go on.

Flo looked at her.

Mavis looked at Flo and said, “I still really don’t know what to do.”

With her fists placed firmly on her ample hips, Flo almost shouted, “She’s 17 for Christ’s sake. You should go around to wherever it is she’s living and bring her back. Take me with you, if you want. One thing’s for sure, at least you can say you’ve done your best for her before it gets too late. That friend is bound to know more about this bloke and where he lives. Make sure you find out.”

George looked up. He was trying to make sense out of what his gran had just said. What’s wrong with Beryl having a boyfriend? He continued to munch on his sandwich and couldn’t be bothered to ask what she was talking about.

Mavis was only a few yards from her front door when she heard her name being called out. She turned. It was Bridget. The local midwife was walking along the pavement, pushing her bike which obviously had a punctured back tyre. Her black holdall, which went everywhere with her, was strapped to the pannier on the back of the bike. Her navy-blue coat was open and it revealed her uniform.

Bridget was looking tired and older than her years. She had helped out with home births for years. If she kept records of all the babies she had delivered in this area, she must by now have a diary the size of an encyclopedia.

“How are you, Mavis? I haven’t seen you about for ages.

Are Flo and the family all right?"

She didn't want this right now.

"We're all fine. Have you just come from a delivery? You look tired."

Bridget stopped and leaned against her bike.

"Yes. I've been out all night and most of the morning with a woman who already has three kids and last night she said this one was going to be her last. Can you believe it, she gave birth to twins. She was as surprised as I was."

She yawned.

"I'm going home to bed now. It was good to see you. By the time your Beryl will need me, she'll find I've retired.

Pulling her coat around her, she went on her way.

Mavis couldn't seem to be able to walk fast enough to reach the place where Ann worked. She was her only hope of getting to know where Beryl might be living.

Her route along the high road took her past Benny's, the café where Ann's mother worked. Mavis kept to the other side of the road so that, hopefully, she wouldn't be noticed. Just as she thought she had passed the window test, Joan came out wiping her hands on a towel. She had seen Mavis.

"Mavis, have you got a minute?"

She was calling out above the noise of the bus which had just gone by.

Mavis's heart sank. She couldn't ignore the woman and had to stop.

Crossing the road, she wasn't sure what she was going to say.

Before she even reached Joan, she had started talking to her. That, she remembered was an annoying habit she had.

"How's your Beryl, then? Ann told me she's got a boyfriend who's going to get her a modelling job and it could even get her into magazines. Does that mean she won't be working at Woolworths anymore?"

Mavis smiled.

"Oh, you don't want to believe everything you hear. It's probably only a fad. I'll speak to her about it tonight."

Joan folded her arms across her chest and frowned.

"I thought she'd moved out."

Mavis was beginning to think she was the only one who didn't know what was going on.

"No. She'll be home soon enough. I've got to go or I'll be late for the shops."

Now she had to get a move on or her trip would be wasted.

The curtain shop was where George had said. It was a small place, not really a shop, just a couple of workrooms down a back alley. It didn't look very inviting and there was a lot of rubbish blowing about in the breeze outside.

She hesitated. Should she knock on the door? The paint was well faded and peeling off in places. Should she just go in?

She could hear the sound of sewing machines being used. There were obviously people in there. She pushed on the door and it opened easily.

As the cold air began to circulate the room, the girls at the machines looked up. They didn't stop working. There were rows of them right across the room. On a side table she could see piles of folded material and a woman in a small side room seemed to be watching through a window. As soon as she saw Mavis, she put down something she was fiddling with and came out.

"Can I help you? Are you here to pick up or deliver?"

Mavis looked across the room but couldn't see Ann anywhere. All the girls were hunched over their machines. She had hoped that if Ann was there, she would have looked up when she came in.

"I hope I'm not intruding but I was looking for Ann, who works here. She is a friend of my daughter and I just needed a quick word with her, if that's all right?"

The woman pursed her lips and was obviously annoyed that Mavis wasn't a trade person.

"I don't usually allow visits in here. It's Ann you said you needed to speak to, is it? I'll let you have a word with her but, only for a minute or two. She's got a lot of work to do."

With that said, she called Ann over from the far side of the room. She had had her back to the door and that's why she hadn't seen Mavis.

Looking round when her name was called, she was very surprised to see Mavis. The woman beckoned for her to come over.

Looking a bit bewildered, she said, "Why are you here? Has there been an accident or something?"

"Only a minute, mind you."

The woman walked away.

Not wanting to alarm her, Mavis said, "No, it's nothing to worry about. I just wondered if you knew where Beryl's boyfriend Tom lives. I need to speak to her and I think she's meeting up with him."

She waited for a response.

Ann looked sheepish.

"She asked me not to say. As well as that, Tom isn't her boyfriend, he is what she calls her agent. He's in charge of what work she gets and how much she gets paid. I think she is sharing a room with at least one other girl and so you don't have to worry about her because she isn't alone."

Mavis was drawing in a deep breath.

"You still haven't told me where she is."

The woman in charge of the machinists was now coming over.

"Ann has to get back to work now, if you don't mind."

As Ann turned away, she said, "I'll tell Beryl you came in and ask her to get in touch with you. Also, she won't be going back to work at Woolworths."

Mavis put her hands up as though she was surrendering to someone. She quietly went over to the door, pulled on the latch and went out. What had just happened?

She stood in the alleyway amongst the litter and felt totally at a loss. In a split second, everything seemed to have changed. She walked home, not registering anything happening around her. If the very devil had appeared before her, she wouldn't have seen him.

She arrived home with Flo waiting on the doorstep. She had a bucket of water by her feet and was holding a cloth which had been wrung out. One of the ladies who used the Church Hall for W.I. meetings was chatting to her. She was always trying to encourage Flo to join them. She had known Flo for years and admired her for the way she was always willing to help people no matter what their problem was.

When she saw Mavis approaching, she was surprised how tired she looked.

“Hello, Mavis. Are you all right? You look as though you have the world’s problems on your shoulders.”

Flo was anxious the conversation didn’t get too personal.

“I was just wiping along the window ledge. I don’t know where all this grit and stuff comes from.” Mavis still hadn’t uttered a word and Flo was getting anxious to know the outcome of the visit to Ann.

Looking at Anthea, Flo said, “I expect you’ve got things to do at the hall. Maybe one of these days I’ll get meself along there and surprise you all.”

“That would be nice, Flo. You would be very welcome.”

With Anthea walking away and Mavis leaning on the wall by the door, Flo picked up her bucket and, swilling the water around, went over to the kerb and emptied the contents down the drain.

“Let’s get in and get the kettle on.”

Sitting in the dim light of the little kitchen, Mavis didn’t know where to start. She wasn’t exactly sure what she had to tell. It hadn’t been a wasted journey but she had come away still not knowing Beryl’s whereabouts.

Beryl sat on the end of the bed trying to work out what was going on. Tom had left her in a couple of rooms upstairs at a friend’s lodgings. She had spent a very fitful night on a very lumpy bed. Most of the clothes she had brought with her were still in the bags she had packed them into. The room had two single beds in it and a chair. The wardrobe next to the window was very old. She had opened it and found there were clothes in it belonging to someone else. She didn’t want to put hers in there as well. This was nothing like her bedroom at home. The lino on the floor was partly covered by a rug whose pattern had been worn away a long time ago. The curtains at the window had been washed but not ironed. A pretty light shade hung down from the ceiling though.

The other room had a sink which was dirty and a small gas cooker which was even dirtier. The table and chairs in the centre of the room were littered with cups and saucers, thankfully washed up. She looked into the cupboard under the sink and had found some Vim and a cloth and that had helped her clean the sink so that she could at least wash her hands and face in it. The only other cupboard which was on the wall contained a tea caddy, half a bottle of milk and a packet of sugar. When she went to the market with Tom, he had said he always took his girls out to the café down the road for breakfast and a meal in the afternoon. She hadn't asked what he meant by 'his girls'.

He said he would be back for her during the morning. What was she to do in the meantime?

When he'd left her yesterday, he'd pulled her close to him and kissed her, his tongue pressing between her lips which gave her a thrill she hadn't experienced before. She loved it when he took her in his arms. He smelt so sweet and fresh. His arms closed around her so tightly, it made her feel safe. She just knew he'd take care of her.

He whispered to her that she would have to stay here only until he had found her work. Then he would set her up in a flat so that she could learn how to be a photographer's model. The other girls would help her to do this. There it was again. 'Other girls'.

Suddenly there was someone coming up the stairs and onto the landing. Her heart raced, and she waited anxiously for

Tom to come into the room.

The door flung open and a woman stood there. She looked about the same age as her mum. She had lots of make-up on with black lines drawn around her eyes which made them seem too big for her face. She was wearing a coat which had a big fur collar and she couldn't see where it ended and her hair began.

She came into the room, her perfume reaching Beryl before she did. It was a sickly smell. She held her hand out, the claw-like fingers stretching to Beryl. Her nails were painted a scarlet colour and Beryl instinctively backed away from them.

She reminded Beryl of a witch in a pantomime.

The woman was like a painted skeleton. She even looked skinny with all her clothes on. Her skin looked like parchment. Her lips were scarlet strips and her hair was pulled back so tightly from her face that first impressions were that she had no hair at all. As Beryl moved backwards, the woman stepped forwards, teetering on stilettos which were like metal rods.

"Tom asked me to look in on you to see if you were all right. He won't be round here until later this afternoon. Are you settled in yet?"

There was a silence.

Beryl found her voice.

"What am I supposed to do? I can't stay here. It's not very nice."

The woman was a bit surprised at this response.

"You'll have to stay here tonight because there isn't room at the flat until tomorrow. One of Tom's girls is going away and won't be back. You can have her space."

Beryl felt very confused. This was not going well. She felt as if she was on a conveyor belt that didn't have an ending.

"Tom will be round about 5 o'clock. He'll collect you and the others so that you can all get something to eat."

Smiling a smile that made her lips seem to part like a scar, she turned and left the room, her stilettos clicking down the stairs and, with a thump, the front door closed.

Beryl was, once again, more confused than ever. This becoming a starlet business wasn't as easy as she had thought it would be.

At Number 48 Francis Road, the afternoon light was starting to fade, and it would only be about another hour before the lights would have to be put on. Annie and Fred always tried to wait until it was absolutely necessary to put them on because that meant winter was approaching and Annie always felt low during the winter months and had to have a tonic from the doctor. She would get herself into a state and not eat properly and so relied on the mixture the doctor gave her called Parishes Food. Fred guessed it was nothing special, but he didn't say anything to Annie as she thought it was good for her.

John and Harry had moved out long ago, with her eldest Harry working on his stall in the market and his brother, John, always finding work doing casual labour. There was still plenty of that about for building work after the war. He was earning good money he told her and was enjoying the good life. They were both settled in lodgings a mile or two away. Annie wouldn't say she had a favourite but John was always in her thoughts because he took chances, but usually, as when he was a boy at school, he'd find a way out of trouble. When they came back from Kent, where they'd been evacuated, they were 12 and 14 and still the centre of attention so far as P.C. Doug was concerned. Any trouble and they were the first two he'd think of. Now they were 21 and 23, he had no reason to think anything had changed.

Their other two boys were teenagers now and, having been brought up by Annie and Fred, they seemed to be staying on the straight and narrow.

Annie was always sad about Sarah. She was now 19 and, after the war, she had asked if she could stay with the couple in Kent who had looked after her when she was evacuated. She loved her mum and dad but liked the life she had living with the couple who had taken her in. Annie and Fred had been to visit her quite a few times and were so proud of the beautiful young girl she had become.

She was a secretary working in the Town Hall in Sidcup. She had a boyfriend who came from a very nice local family and everything seemed to be working out for her. Annie and Fred considered Sarah's story was one of the good ones that came out of the war years.

The shadows in the kitchen were getting longer and so Fred heaved himself out of his old comfy chair by the fireplace and flicked the light switch. The news would be on soon on the wireless and so he started tuning it in, the whistles it made still making him smile. It was as though it was summoning the B.B.C. to liven up.

"I don't suppose there's going to be anything new on the news, love. The lunchtime one was about it would soon be time to change the clocks for winter. We know that anyway. It looks as though we are going to have a nice quiet evening with the boys out."

The calm silence was suddenly broken. Someone was thumping hard on the front door. Three hard knocks. Why didn't, whoever it was, use the knocker?

"Who the hell is that this time of the day?"

Fred looked at Annie with a worried expression, his frown almost closing his eyes. She automatically straightened her apron when she stood up.

On opening the front door, Fred was confronted by a large muscular bloke he didn't recognize. Fred wasn't a small man anyway, but this bloke towered over him.

"Are you Fred Greening?"

Fred stood squarely in the doorway.

"Who's asking?"

"I think I'd better say what I've got to say inside. I don't think it's something to talk about on the step."

Feeling threatened by the bloke's attitude, Fred pulled the door closer to himself.

"Are you selling something because, if you are, you're wasting your time, mate. This time of the day I don't expect a stranger to be coming round."

The bloke's expression changed.

"If you want the street to know your business, I am quite happy to say what I've got to say on your doorstep. You know how walls have ears and there's bound to be people watching from behind net curtains. I don't know your street, but I bet it's the same as mine and I'm from South London."

Fred couldn't imagine what this bloke wanted, and he continued to stand his ground. Annie was calling from the kitchen.

Not wanting to alarm her, her said, "You'd better come

into the front room."

The bloke stepped inside while Fred closed the door.

Showing him into the front room, he flicked the light on and quietly closed the door behind him. He didn't suggest they sat down because he wanted to hear what this bloke wanted and then get him out of the house. They both stood in front of the fireplace.

Fred almost glared at the bloke and said, "So what's this about?"

"I want to speak to your son, but I don't know where he lives. I found out where you were though and that's why I'm here."

Fred moved from one foot to the other and stuck his hands into his trouser pockets. He was feeling cautious now and wasn't sure what he was going to hear.

"Who do you mean? I've got four sons."

"John, that's the one."

The bloke seemed to straighten and appeared bigger than when Fred first saw him.

"The little sod has got my daughter pregnant."

Suddenly, the room seemed to have had the air sucked out of it.

The door handle turned and Annie came in.

"Is everything all right, Fred?"

"Go and put the kettle on, love. We'll be through in a minute."

Fred was a bit lost for words and said the first thing that came into his head.

"Well, he never told us he had a girlfriend and he's never brought her round here to meet us."

Fred was thinking, it's bloody Johnny again. Well, this is one scrape he's not going to be able to get out of.

They went into the kitchen. Annie was standing by the table.

"What's going on, Fred?"

"Johnny has got himself into a bit of bother, love."

Looking at the bloke, he said, "I never asked your name."

"Jim Venables."

Fred gestured for him to sit down. Annie was pouring the tea.

"It looks like you're going to be a grandmother, love."

Annie went visibly rigid.

"What are you talking about?"

"It's Johnny. He's done it this time. This bloke, Jim Venables, says he's got his daughter pregnant."

Seconds passed, which seemed like minutes and then Annie, in her protective manner, said the worst thing she could.

"How do you know the baby is John's?"

Jim Venables drew in a deep breath. Leaning forward over the table, he said, "Are you saying my girl is in the habit of sleeping with anyone?"

Fred could see where this was going.

"Right, before anything more is said that we're all going to regret, why don't I get Johnny round here tomorrow and we can all find out what's been going on. If you can bring your daughter round here tomorrow night, we can get things sorted. I think

that would be for the best."

Annie, once again, found her interest stirred.

"How far gone is she?"

Fred was amazed that she seemed so calm. He wondered if she had thought that someday it would be a problem to be dealt with.

Jim Venables sat back on his chair.

"She tells me she is two months and so I want this wedding to be before she starts showing. There's going to be a wedding, you mark my words."

There was no more to be said tonight and it was agreed that they would all have a meeting tomorrow in their front room.

The evening was spent in subdued silence by Annie while Fred went round to where Johnny was living with Harry and the meeting was arranged. Johnny showed no sign of surprise or panic.

The next morning Annie felt she just had to speak to someone she could trust and, of course, that would be Flo. As soon as Fred had left for work, she made her way along to see her. The front door was ajar. Calling out, she went in and along to the kitchen. Mavis was in the scullery washing up.

Looking up, she said, "Oh, I thought I heard someone come in. I thought it was Mum. She's just popped along the street for a minute. Did you want to speak to her? She won't be long."

Annie had started off the morning feeling quite calm, having mulled things over in her mind during the night. Now she was feeling not so good.

"Yes, I was going to ask her about something but, on second thoughts, you've got your own problems to sort out with Beryl running off with the boyfriend and so I shouldn't bother her with my problem."

Mavis stopped washing up.

"Where did you hear that about Beryl?"

"Nel, your neighbour, told me. She said she's given her job up as well."

Just then Flo came shuffling into the kitchen.

"Annie, what are you doing here?"

Grimacing, she pulled a chair out from the table and sat down.

"We've had a bit of news which I need to speak to you about. Fred doesn't know I'm here."

Flo moved closer.

"Well, I'm all ears. Don't keep me in suspense."

By the time Annie had told the story, she had embellished it a bit. Jim Venables was now sounding like a bloke you didn't mess with.

Flo drew in a deep breath. "It doesn't surprise me, Annie, and it shouldn't surprise you. Your John has always been the one to bring trouble home."

She paused, sinking her hand inside her jumper to adjust her bra strap.

"The one thing you've got to make sure of is that this girl, whoever she is, knows it's John's baby. Can he definitely say she's only been seeing him?"

Before any more could be said, Flo put her finger to her lips

"Keep the conversation low. I'm sure these bloody walls have ears. I bet Nel is pressing a glass to the wall at this very moment."

They all smiled.

After mulling a few more points over, including what to do about a wedding tea and where it would be held, Annie left so that she could dust and hoover the front room for the meeting tonight. She'd get the best china out as well.

CHAPTER THREE

Beryl stood by the sink looking through the grubby pane of glass at the gardens which ran along the back of these houses in this street. They were all like wasted strips of ground, each one separated by either broken wooden fencing or anything else that would mark a boundary. Most of them were only used for drying washing or storing out of use bikes and other children's toys that had been discarded. This whole street, she had been told, was due for demolition and its tenants had been promised fine new homes in one of the new towns that were springing up in Essex. They would have kitchens with modern cookers and refrigerators and also a bathroom with a toilet in it.

She thought of the secure home she had grown up in and the garden her mum had cultivated. She had dug over the soil and planted marigolds and gladioli. Wallflowers and golden rod completed the patchwork of colour during the summer months making it look like a harlequin's outfit.

If her mum and gran decide to move into one of the new houses, their little garden would become a wasteland like the ones she was looking at now.

She wondered what people's gardens were like in America. The magazines she bought all showed the sun shining and everyone looking happy. The stars' homes had swimming pools in their gardens and exotic plants surrounding their houses.

The starlets all had hair that was set in waves and when they smiled, their teeth glowed with whiteness. Tom had told her that when she let her hair hang loosely it made her look very pretty and he also liked her smile. Perhaps that's why he thought he could make her into a model.

Her thoughts were jarred to a halt when she heard the front door slam. Banging footsteps were coming up the stairs and there in the doorway was Tom. She felt so relieved at seeing him she immediately rushed over.

"Steady on, girl. You'll knock me over."

Standing back, he said, "I'm taking you and a couple of the other girls out to eat and so look lively."

Beryl was a bit surprised at his cool response to her greeting.

"They're waiting downstairs."

Her first thoughts were; she didn't look or feel very glamorous. I bet his other girls have had time to get ready.

"I need to do my hair and make-up first and I am still wearing yesterday's clothes."

"Don't worry about that. We're only going to the café at the end of the street."

Somehow, she felt disappointed at hearing that. Even when she and Ann went out just to a coffee bar, they made themselves look nice.

Once in the café, Tom got them some sandwiches and cakes together with mugs of tea. Beryl only then realized how hungry she was as she hadn't eaten anything since yesterday.

The girls introduced themselves. Martine was very tall with long blonde hair and had the bluest eyes Beryl had ever seen. Grace had black curly hair with Latino features about her which made her look very sultry.

"This is Donna. She is our latest model and will rely on you two to teach her how to pose."

He was smiling the whole time he was saying this.

"She can move into the flat with you two now that Jane has left."

Between eating and drinking the tea, Beryl asked, "Where has Jane gone then?"

Tom was quick with an answer.

"She had family trouble and so she has gone to live on the coast."

Putting the mug of tea down, Beryl said, "I'd like to live on the coast sometime. I love going to Southend."

The others looked at each other.

Almost choking on his sandwich, Tom said, "Oh, she's gone a lot further away than that. I offered to help her but she wouldn't let me and so I took her up to Paddington Station this morning and put her on a train to Cornwall."

Beryl looked surprised.

"I couldn't go that far. Not on me own."

"It's where she wanted to go. As far away as possible, she said."

Beryl was puzzled.

"Didn't you say she had family problems? Wasn't she going home then?"

Before she could ask any more questions, Beryl sensed she shouldn't be talking about someone she didn't know.

"Right then. Are we finished here?"

Standing up, Tom gestured to the other girls to lead the

way and they all left the café.

"We need to pick your stuff up and get over to the flat."

Beryl sat on the back seat of the car. Martine sat next to her and Grace was in the front seat next to Tom. She didn't know what she was feeling. Was it excitement, fear or the realization that this was finally it? She was being taken into the world of a photographer's model and everything from now on would be wonderful.

She gazed out of the window at how ordinary everything looked. So far, her new life was only a dream and, once she had been taught how to pose and make herself look special, she would be able to earn lots of money and could then visit her mum and gran and show them what she had achieved.

She worried about the clothes she had brought with her. Would they be good enough? She worried about the make-up she had bought at the chemist when Ann was with her. Was it the right kind?

She had painted her fingernails with a colour she thought was nice but now, sitting in silence in the car, she looked at them and thought the colour looked cheap.

Martine and Grace had not spoken since they left the café. She got the impression they had made this journey many times before. Beryl had hoped they would be making some sort of conversation about the flat they were all going to share.

She could smell the lotion that Tom had put on his face which he called after shave. It wafted around the car. She didn't know anyone else who used that. It must be special.

The journey didn't take long. They had passed through lots of streets she didn't recognize. They had sped past huge department stores she had never been in and a street with lots of stalls lining it selling unusual things she hadn't seen before. She only knew stalls which sold vegetables and fruit or materials and clothes. Everywhere she looked was like seeing a new world and, yet, she was still in London where she had lived all her life.

The car slowed down and stopped, and Beryl saw they were outside a tall building which was obviously what people call a block of flats. She peered out, looking up at

all the windows.

Grace opened her door and stepped out. Martine looked at Beryl.

"Get your bags out of the boot and we can go up."

It sounded more like an order than a request.

Without a word, Beryl took her now crumpled bags out and put them on the pavement.

Martine said, "Luckily, the lift is still working and so we can use that."

Beryl didn't really understand. The only time she had been in a lift was when her uncle took the family out to a hotel and the place they were going to eat in was on another floor. If the place she was going to be living in needed a lift to get to it, she was beginning to feel a bit special.

The building was very quiet. The lights in the corridors were dull and cast shadows as they had at school. She immediately felt disappointed.

The lift was metal and grubby. They all stepped into it. It was now crowded, and she didn't want to put her heavy bags down because the floor was in a state. The alarm bells were ringing in her head. This was not how it's supposed to be.

There was a difficult silence.

She felt the lift noisily and reluctantly dragging itself up the shaft.

After passing three floors, the clattering of the lift chains stopped. With a silent jolt, the doors opened and they all stepped out.

The passageway they had stepped into was like a tunnel of plain green walls with several doors along one side of it. There were no signs of life. No bustling sounds. No welcoming mood. The building seemed like an empty shell.

As they made their way into the gloom, suddenly there was a faint sound of music playing, probably from a radio behind one of the closed doors. That was the only sign that there were people in this building. She felt almost relieved.

They stopped at a door marked No. 12. Tom reached into his pocket for a key and opened the door.

Martine pushed the door open and went in. Grace pushed passed Beryl and then turning, beckoned to her to follow.

She was in a living room which seemed, at first glance, bright and clean. She put her bags down with a bit of a thud.

Martine glared at her.

"You can sleep in that room over there."

She was pointing her bony finger towards a closed door.

"The bath and toilet are in here," she said.

"Leave it as you find it. I can't stand people who make a mess in there and don't clean it up. While you're working for Tom, we're the ones you've got to live with. Now that Jane has gone, we should set out some rules for the place."

Beryl was feeling panic rising. Why was she living with these two people and not living with Tom? She wondered what they meant by rules. That's what she was escaping from.

Grace went into the little space in the corner of the room which looked like a kitchen. There were cupboards along the wall and she could see a kettle, a sink and a cooker. It reminded her of the inside of her aunt's caravan and she hated that.

Without even turning around, Martine called out to her to get her things into the bedroom.

"You'll be busy tomorrow. We'll be over at the salon and your make-up and hair will need to be done."

Beryl stood her ground all of a sudden. She hadn't made a fuss up until now. She felt she had been spoken to very rudely and they were not being nice to her. She was, after all, the one Tom had chosen to be a model.

"I've brought my own make-up and I can do my own hair. I know how it goes."

With a positive gesture, she picked her bags up and took them into the bedroom.

It didn't look any different from any other bedroom. She had expected it would be special.

Unpacking her things, she found that she was sharing a wardrobe with somebody else and she didn't like that. It was the same as when she was in that filthy flat.

Calling out, she said, "What clothes will I want for tomorrow?"

Martine's reply was a bit strange.

"You can put anything you like on. The clothes you'll be wearing for the shoot are already at the salon."

That night, Beryl lay in the strange and uncomfortable bed looking at shadows dancing on the walls. The curtains in the room were so thin that the lamppost lights outside reflected across the darkness. She had hardly slept. She worried she would look awful in the morning. She wasn't used to being away from home on her own, but this was going to be something she was going to have to get used to. There were now more unfamiliar noises echoing around these flats at night than there were during daylight hours.

Having eventually fallen asleep, she awoke with a start, finding Grace hovering over her with a cup of tea.

"Drink this and have something to eat. Tom will be picking us up in an hour."

There were so many questions she wanted to ask. She had brought some savings with her, but she didn't know if she should offer some rent money which Tom had mentioned. He had told her that if she was a success at modelling, she would be given presents by the people who liked her photos. That, she thought, sounded good.

She felt relieved when Tom arrived. He gathered her up in his arms and kissed her. "Let's get you over to the salon. The girls will do your make-up and hair and then we'll decide what you should wear for your first photos."

Beryl pulled away from him.

"Will I be wearing someone else's clothes? I'm not sure I would like that."

Smiling, he said, "Don't you worry about it. I'm sure you'll like them."

Why did she feel there was something he wasn't telling her? Surely, having your photo taken shouldn't be this involved. Also, why were the girls always with her?

Her hadn't told her about them before. Why would they need to help her with make-up and hair?

She was trying to control her thoughts and anxieties but it

didn't seem to be working.

"I'll tell you what. Why don't I drive you over to the salon, just the two of us? I can pick the girls up later. What do you think?"

Beryl liked that idea. She would feel happier about that.

"Oh, yes. I just want to be with you, Tom."

"Let me have a word with Martine and Grace and then we can go."

After a strangely whispered conversation with Martine, he came over to her.

"Time's getting on. Let's get down to the car."

Sitting next to Tom as the car sped along, Beryl was beginning to calm down. She had told Ann that, once things had settled down a bit, she would write to her. She knew Ann wouldn't give her mum and gran any information about her whereabouts. She trusted Ann to keep all her secrets, no matter what they were. That, she was to discover, would nearly cost her, her life.

Drawing up at a parade of shops, Tom looked at her and said, "This is where I have to leave you. The photographer is waiting upstairs in the salon. You can meet him at the top of the stairs where he'll show you in."

He pointed to door which appeared to be between two shops.

Looking at her, he said, "In you go."

With one last look at him, she got out of the car and went through the narrow door. The stairs were immediately in front of her and had no covering on them. They were just bare boards. Looking up, she saw someone standing at the top of them. A wooden hand rail ran along the wall. It was all so silent, despite the fact there was a bustling world just outside the door.

Beryl's grip on her make-up bag was so tight, her nails were digging into the palm of her hand. She suddenly felt scared and alone.

Looking up at the figure looming in the light ahead of her, she realized she hadn't even been told the photographer's name. She stayed rooted to the spot as though any move she made would make her lose balance.

"It's Donna, isn't it? Do come up. I've been waiting for you."

He held his hand out and beckoned to her. He seemed quite young and reminded her of a friend of Ann's. That seemed all right in her mind.

"Tom has just dropped me off. I didn't know I'd be on me own."

"Well, if you come up here, you won't be, will you."

She couldn't make her mind up if he was being sarcastic.

With that, he turned and went into the room behind him.

Beryl climbed the steep stairs, her stiletto's clicking on the bare boards. At the top, the door was open to a room that had lots of tripods and camera equipment in it. Curiously, there was also a couch, a small bar in one corner with lots of bottles of alcohol, a bit like her uncle had in his house, and a metal clothes rack holding all kinds of clothes. Near the curtain-less window she could see a wide shelf crowded with pots of make-up and lots of hair brushes. A mirror which had been placed over the shelf had coloured lights around the edge of it.

An enormous mirror which stood on the floor against the wall covered most of the far wall.

"My name's Justin. The girls will be here soon to get you looking right. I'm not sure what Tom wants for your first session. He may just want shots to see how you photograph."

Beryl felt very confused.

"What am I supposed to do?"

Pointing to the couch, he said, "Just sit over there until the others arrive. I hope they won't be long. I've got another two shoots to do today."

Tom was back at the flat and bounding up the stairs two at a time. Martine was waiting in the small kitchen area, her long thin fingers holding a cigarette, the smoke spiralling up and disappearing.

Grace was sitting at the table tapping her fingernails in a monotonous way as though in time with some silent tune.

Looking over at Tom, she said, "So what's next? We're wasting our time while you're pandering to little Miss Special. I, for one, have got other things I can be doing."

Her tone was filling the room with anger.

"OK. OK. We're going to have to get some photos done today. I've got customers waiting for new girls. I need you two to start the ball rolling by getting her made-up and ready. I thought we might go for the prim and proper look to start with. You know, all buttoned up and don't touch. We'll see how she looks like that and I also think it will relax her a bit. She's definitely not ready yet for the scanty things."

With the atmosphere evaporating into work mode, both girls followed Tom down to the car.

Back at the salon, Justin was getting very tetchy. He knew how Tom and the girls worked and he also felt they had made a mistake with this latest 'model'.

He had been busying himself with the equipment while observing Beryl without her realizing. She didn't look as though she was going to be any good.

The door downstairs banged shut and the sound of people getting nearer gave him a sense of relief.

Tom was first in.

He was smiling and seemed very relaxed.

"I'm glad you've met Justin. He'll be able to show you how to pose once the girls have made you look like a model. That'll be good won't it? I just know you're going to be great."

Beryl, still sitting on the sofa, smiled as though she was convinced that her decision to leave home had been the right thing to do. No one in her family had been famous before.

At No. 4 Francis Road the letterbox clattered. The postman had delivered a letter. Mavis wondered who would be writing to her. She didn't get much post. She hoped it wasn't bad news, perhaps about a friend. Flo always said bad news travels fast and so it couldn't be bad news because a letter would take too long. The only telephone in the street was the one at the pub, but that was only for emergencies.

Picking the letter up from the mat, she could see it was a local postmark. The address was typewritten.

Flo was out, and so Mavis sat down at the kitchen table and used the butter knife to slit along the seal of the envelope. She opened the folded paper.

It was a letter from Woolworths. The printed letterhead was black and bold.

Mrs Davenport had written to say that they could not continue to hold Beryl's job open for her and they had given the job to someone else. She was very sorry to have to do this but, the manager had insisted the position was filled as soon as possible.

She asked Mavis to let Beryl know.

Mavis put the letter down. The only sound was her own breathing which was strangely loud. She seemed to be drawing in long breaths and sighing as she breathed out. She sat there and was still sitting there when Flo came in.

Bundling into the kitchen clutching the shopping bag which looked about to burst, Flo was glad to be back from shopping.

"I thought the handle was going to give up on this before I got home but, luckily, it didn't. I've had this for so long, I can't remember where I bought it. Anyway, the corner shop had the stuff I wanted and so I didn't have to go up the high road."

With a heave and a thump, the bag was hoisted onto the table. It was then that she noticed the open letter.

"Who's been writing to us?"

Mavis picked the letter up and pushed it towards Flo.

"Beryl's lost her job."

Flo read the letter.

"Well, I'm not surprised. If she's been having days off that we didn't know about, it was on the cards they wouldn't put up with that."

She read the letter again.

"What's this Mrs Davenport like? Does she have any kiddies?"

Mavis looked up.

"No. She said they hadn't been blessed."

Flo put the letter down.

Mavis was sitting silently at the table. She felt as though she must have done something wrong to have this happen to her. Her mother seemed to be, as usual, taking it all in her stride. How could she?

At Annie and Fred's house, Annie was standing in front of the dressing table mirror. She patted her hair and was happy how she looked. Her best frock was colourful and the silver bow brooch which was her best one, looked nice on the collar of it. Yes, she was happy to meet this person who was having Johnny's baby. She was going to be friendly towards her but had a few questions she wanted answered.

To many people she might have seemed an unassuming tenant in this street but, as was very often the case, she was a people watcher and observed their reactions when things started going wrong. She was also a listener and, on her many visits to the market, she picked up on conversations which the barrow boys offered to their fellow stallholders when a decision had to be made about personal problems. They showed no embarrassment by discussing anything openly in the market, from sexual liaisons to debt problems.

As Annie moved slowly between the stalls, she sometimes felt she was eavesdropping but, these people were so up front about what was on their minds, they almost seemed to be offering a situation up and were waiting for a solution.

She stood back from the dressing table mirror and decided that the meeting tonight could go one way or the other without anything said by her or Fred. This was going to be a matter for Johnny to take the lead in and he mustn't feel he had to marry the girl. This was a lifetime decision he was going to make.

The scene was set, and the front room looked at its best.

Fred had lit a fire in there and the flickering flames lifted your spirits while their warmth welcomed you to them.

Fred felt confident he would be in charge in his own house. He looked at the clock on the mantelpiece. It had stood there for at least 20 years ticking away unnoticed. Now it was the centre of attention as the time slipped closer to 7 o'clock when the meeting was to take place.

Fred turned and left the room, closing the door behind him.

The silence of the moment was abruptly broken. Someone was knocking on the front door and calling through the letterbox. What was happening?

Annie appeared at the top of the stairs.

"Did you hear that, Fred? Are we being burgled or something?"

Fred opened the front door and found Routine Rosie standing back on the pavement looking up to the sky. She was pointing to the rooftops. It was only then that Fred noticed his neighbour was also out on the pavement.

"What the hell's going on?"

Routine Rosie stood back into the road.

"I was on me usual walk when I saw a lot of smoke coming from your chimney stack and then there were sparks going up into the air."

Fred's neighbour was getting very agitated.

"I was about to knock because I could smell smoke in me kitchen. I hope your place isn't on fire or something."

Annie appeared in the doorway.

"What's going on, Fred?"

Looking outside, she could see there were quite a few

people standing around in the road now, including Flo and Mavis.

Someone in the gathering crowd shouted out, "Do you need the fire brigade?"

Fred then realized that the chimney must have been blocked up when he lit the fire in the front room. It was probably those bloody pigeons dropping stuff down it.

Rushing back into the house, as soon as he opened the door to the front room, he was engulfed in smoke. His neighbour had followed him in and went straight to the kitchen and filled a saucepan with water. Rushing back along the smoke-filled passage, he rushed into the front room, spilling some of the water in his haste. Throwing it in the direction of the fireplace, there was a sizzling sound as the flames were put out. As the smoke cleared, Fred and his neighbour started coughing and rubbing their eyes.

Shifty Sam appeared from the smoke-filled passage where he had gone in to see what was going on. Annie was standing near the front door.

"You were lucky, love. It could have spread next door and further along. The roof voids on these old places don't give you any protection. Me and Jim have done plenty of removals in places like this."

Out on the street, Flo and Mavis were talking to their neighbour, Nel.

It was Nel that was more than curious.

"What on earth made Fred light a fire in the front room? He only does that at Christmas." She was directing the question at anyone who could give her an answer.

Annie was now standing among the gathering of

neighbours.

Before Flo could get to her, the familiar bulk of P.C. Doug came down the road on his bike. Parking it up against the wall, he started peering at the rooftops.

"What are we all looking at, then?"

Shifty Sam went over to him.

"You're not usually around here this time of the day."

P.C. Doug usually knew what was going on almost before it happened, and he was curious.

"Am I missing something?"

"Fred's chimney was alight just now. No damage done though."

P.C. Doug took his helmet off. His thick thatch of brown hair seemed to spread out once released. He'd grown up in this street. He'd always wanted to join the police. He knew all the local villains and who to look out for when there was trouble. He'd been to school with most of them. Fred's boys used to be a first port of call when they were younger but now they seemed to have stayed on the right side of the law, so far as he knew.

With the evening light now descending and with all the lights on in the houses, some of the tenants had brought chairs out and were sitting drinking tea and chatting while all the commotion was going on. The street had taken on the look of a party.

He looked over his shoulder at all the familiar faces milling around. One of the people standing next to him was a chap that had lived in this street for many years. Looking at him, he said, "It doesn't take much for them all to find an excuse to get out does it?"

He decided that as no one had been injured, he would make his way home now that his shift had ended.

Flo went over to Annie and could see she was in a bit of a state.

"Let's get you inside, dear, and you can sort yourself out."

Before they could go in, a van pulled up. They both stared at it.

Annie's mouth fell open.

"Oh, Flo, this is terrible. They're our visitors."

As Flo guided her inside, Annie stopped in the doorway of the front room. Peering in, she gasped. There was no damage, but the whole room, furniture and everything, seemed to have lost its sparkle. The smoke had left the place with a smell she wouldn't forget.

Flo was trying to push her into the kitchen and away from it all.

On the street, Jim Venables, his wife and daughter were emerging from the van.

Further along, John was sauntering down the street, whistling the usual tune which always heralded his approach. This, he was thinking, was going to be some meeting.

Fred looked up and saw him and was thankful he was actually on time.

Fred was standing on the pavement by the window. The front door was fully open and an alarming smell of burning was coming from the place.

His face was grey and his freshly washed and ironed shirt was now bearing the marks of soot.

The neighbours were still milling about in the street, even One-leg Len and his wife, Edna. Those standing near them were politely making excuses to move away because, as usual, Edna was giving off a smell that made everyone wonder if she ever washed.

Nel was keen to know who these strangers were. She knew they weren't relatives of Fred and Annie. There was nothing she liked better than a mystery. She even got books from the library which involved mysteries. She always read the first three chapters and then the last two. She couldn't wait to find what the answer was in the story.

Jim Venables, his wife and daughter were still standing by the van. John had now reached the little party and smiled at his girlfriend.

"What's been going on?"

Nel said, "There's been a fire but it's all sorted now."

John smiled. "You can't blame me for that one. I wasn't even here."

His smile said it all.

Nel thought, he'll never change. He's always been a cocky little sod. You'd never know he was Annie and Fred's son. He was nothing like them.

Jim Venables stepped forward. His wife was looking a bit alarmed. She was wearing a very well-cut suit which showed off her slim figure. A gold necklace and earrings completed the look. What on earth was she thinking when confronted by all

this chaos nobody could imagine. She pulled her daughter closer to her.

Fred finally came alive.

"As you can see, we've had a bit of a problem. It might be better if we can postpone our meeting until tomorrow.

It was agreed that they would come round again the next evening. They could see that Annie and Fred were very upset at what had happened and, no doubt, they would be hearing about it on their next visit.

John stepped forward and sidled up to his girlfriend, whispering to her. She was a pretty little thing. Fred pulled John away from her and shot him a look that John knew only too well from the past. Don't touch!

Flo had calmed Annie down as best she could and convinced her that it wasn't the end of the world. She would pop in tomorrow morning and, once Fred had arranged for the chimney to be swept, the two of them could give the front room a good clean.

The real casualty of this little episode was Nel who hadn't been able to find out exactly who the visitors were, although she was putting two and two together and guessing it was trouble that John had brought home.

Flo turned to Mavis and said, "I've told Annie I'll help her get the front room cleaned up. They've got those people coming around again tomorrow. If that's the young girl John needs to marry, they're going to need some help with the wedding tea as well as everything else. There's a lot to sort out.

The next morning, Flo wrapped her hair up in a turban, got out a collection of dusters from the cupboard under the stairs and picked up her metal bucket. Her apron needed washing anyway and so that would do for now. Looking like a household warrior, she marched along the street to Annie's house.

The mess looked worse in daylight. Fred had gone to work

leaving them to it, thankful the worst was over.

By early afternoon they had the room looking ready for guests. They'd earned a rest and a cup of tea. No sooner had they sat down at the kitchen table when a knock on the front door broke the mood.

Looking at Annie, Flo said, "Who the hell can that be? Are you expecting anyone?"

Flo was very put out that their few minutes of rest had been interrupted. Annie pulled herself up from the kitchen chair.

"I'll see who it is. Perhaps it's someone wanting to help with the clean-up. They've probably waited until now, hoping it's all been done."

Flo smiled. At least Annie was getting her sense of humour back.

Her weary tread along the passage seemed to take ages before she reached the front door. As she opened it, she drew in a sharp breath. It was one of the barmaids from the pub.

"Are you Mrs Greening?"

Annie felt she didn't want to say 'yes'.

CHAPTER FOUR

Flo could hear a muffled voice but couldn't recognize it. She stood up and went to the kitchen doorway. Looking towards the front door she could see Annie but couldn't see who she was talking to.

The early afternoon light was casting shadows. Flo didn't like shadows. They always belonged to trouble. Annie gasped, her hand held up to her face. She was obviously listening to something the young girl was saying to her and seemed distressed.

Flo could only hear a bit of the muffled conversation but, what she did hear loud and clear, was the word 'hospital'. With her curiosity rising, she had to find out what was going on. After all, she was here to help Annie.

"What's going on, Annie? What's happening?"

Annie turned, leaving the door wide open and started walking back to the kitchen. She was just staring ahead of her. She hadn't said anything. She seemed struck dumb.

Flo pushed past her and went up to the young girl.

"What's happened? Is it something to do with Fred? Has he had an accident at work?"

The young girl stepped back from the doorway, almost afraid she was going to be grabbed by Flo.

"I've come from the pub because they've had a phone call from the hospital to say John Greening is there. They asked us to let you know and that's what I'm here for. I don't know any more than that."

It was obvious she wanted to get back to the pub as soon as possible and she was already starting to turn away.

Flo sighed.

"OK. I'll take it from here. Thanks for letting us know."

She stepped back and closed the door. She'd just reached the kitchen when there was another knock on the door.

"Who the hell! What's going on here?"

Flo looked at Annie and the two of them looked up to the ceiling and drew in a breath.

The knock sounded again followed by a loud call through the rattled letterbox.

"Are you two all right in there? I saw that Jane from the pub at your door and she only comes out in an emergency."

It then went silent. Flo was almost spitting with fury.

"Would you believe it. This news is only minutes old and that old cow from up the road already knows something's up."

Annie showed no sign of being surprised that Nel was on the case. She almost had an observation post in her front room window. Flo was incensed. She opened the door to her with a stony face and said, "We've got to go out and so there's no use you hanging around here. Now, get lost."

She slammed the door shut with such force it made Annie jump.

"Get your coat on, girl. We'll go around to Shifty Sam. He'll take us up to the hospital to find out what's going on."

Annie had never felt so scared in her life. This was worse than an air raid during the war. At least then you knew what was happening.

She was getting flustered.

"I ought to leave a note for Fred. If he comes home and I'm not here, he won't know where I am."

Grabbing Annie from the chair, Flo said, "There's no use leaving a note because we don't know what's happened. Anyway, if we can get to the hospital quickly, at least

we'll be able to find out what John has done to himself."

Pushing Annie out of the kitchen, there was barely time for her to grab her bag and key. Flo then realized she was still wearing her wrap-around apron and her hair was still encased in the turban. Even she was getting worked up now.

They made their way around to Shifty Sam's yard, hoping he'd be there. The two of them must have looked a funny pair with Flo bouncing along clutching poor Annie by the arm, almost lifting her off her feet in haste. They didn't want to be stopped by anyone or that would mean a delay in getting to Sam's place. They were both silently praying he'd be there. If he wasn't, they'd have to get the bus to the hospital and that would take a while.

As they turned into Sam's street, they could hear an engine revving up. Flo looked at Annie and grinned. "We're in luck."

Looking up at the two of them, Sam was very surprised to see them.

"Have you got something you want shifted? I could do with some work. Good job I've got me old cart, because the lorry's playing up."

Annie's heart sank for a minute.

Flo stepped forward.

"Annie's had a bit of bad news. We heard one of her lot's

been taken to hospital in a hurry. Can you give us a lift?"

She didn't want to mention John's name because Sam had had a few run-ins with him in the past. John was very volatile.

Sam immediately stopped fiddling with the lorry and said, "Get in girls. Of course, I'll take you."

Flo almost pushed Annie onto the grubby seat and then got in beside her. Sam tried to make conversation, but his passengers hadn't spoken. The lorry smelt of petrol and stale food. Obviously, Sam never cleaned the inside of it and, it seemed as though it was where he ate the pies he liked during the day. The smell of onions was awful. Annie just wished he'd stop talking and concentrate on the driving. She was nervous enough as it was.

Her mind was racing through all sorts of possible problems. Had John been injured at work on the building site? Yes, he must have been. He never could take the advice from his mates about being careful when dealing with all the machinery and equipment on those sites. The site foreman was always pushing them to do more.

She heaved a visible sigh of relief as they pulled into the car park at the hospital.

As she got out of the lorry, she looked at Sam and said, "Can you hang around until we find out if John can come home with us?"

As soon as she said that, Sam's attitude changed. He didn't like the bloke and wasn't surprised that he was the one in trouble. There was even a rumour on the street that he'd got a girl pregnant.

"I'm sorry, love, but I've got to get back. I've got to get me lorry sorted."

He left the two of them standing in the hospital doorway.

The hospital building was so unfamiliar to them and they didn't want to be here.

Despite all the obvious activity with people making their way along corridors, which seemed to go on forever, and telephones ringing, the islands of chairs, as they approached the reception area, seemed to be the only quiet place, although the floors seemed to echo with every step taken.

A long shelf-like desk they approached had the only person they could see sitting behind it. Annie remembered the headmaster's desk at school which seemed just as important. She stopped walking and held back.

Flo pushed forward.

"Can you help us? We've heard that my friend's son has been brought in. Where do we go to find him?"

The woman behind the desk didn't look up. She merely uttered, "Name?"

"My name's Florence Taylor and this is Annie Greening."

The woman finally looked up and raised her eyebrows.

"I need the name of the person who has been brought in."

Her voice was sounding impatient, although she didn't seem to have much to do. She leaned forward and stared directly at Flo. There was silence. Flo instinctively didn't like her.

"It's John Greening."

Still looking at Flo, she said, "When was he brought in?"

Flo was now getting the hump with her. She made them feel they were being a nuisance and the woman ought to be more helpful to them. If this is what the talked about NHS was going to be like, they ought to employ nicer people. She was getting more annoyed.

"We don't know what time he was brought in and we don't know what his injury is but, I can tell you this, we are not going anywhere until we get some answers."

The woman then looked at Annie.

"Are you a relative?"

Annie came out from behind Flo.

"I'm his mother."

The woman shuffled some papers in front of her

Pointing to some chairs which were part of the island in the centre of the room, she said, "Please wait over there and I will find out where your son has been taken."

She left the desk and went into a room behind her. Flo and Annie strolled across the room and sat down. They both sat there in silence. Neither of them could think of anything to say.

Within minutes the woman returned. Flo and Annie went back to the desk.

"John Greening you say."

All this repeating stuff was getting on Flo's nerves.

"So, what's wrong with him then?"

The woman stared directly at her. Pointing to the left of her, she said, "If you go down that corridor to X-ray, they will be able to tell you. The report says he came in himself at half past ten. There's nothing more I can tell you."

Grabbing hold of Annie's arm, Flo hurried her along the sterile corridor, reading all the signs aloud for the different departments. With curtains pulled across doorways and nurses scurrying around corners, the whole scene resembled one of those *Carry On* films they had seen at the pictures but, this wasn't funny. The sign for X-ray and an arrow, that's what they had been looking for. There it was.

Following the sign, they were confronted with yet another set of chairs and a door with a warning sign on it not to enter.

Flo was getting very annoyed now. She sat the silent and confused Annie down on one of the chairs and decided to continue along the corridor until she found someone who could give her some answers. Annie didn't like the fuss Flo was making and felt almost embarrassed.

Just as she was passing one of the curtained areas, John appeared in front of her with a surprised look on his face. He looked as though he had been in a fight, his clothes disheveled and his right hand heavily bandaged. He was holding a loose sling in his other hand. He looked directly at her.

Flo stared hard at him. "What the hell has happened to you? Your poor mother is worried sick." Turning and pointing behind her, she said, "She's sitting in that waiting area along there."

She was pointing to where Annie had been left. The sudden silence was awful.

A nurse caught up with him.

"You'll need to see your own doctor in a couple of weeks so make an appointment with him. In the meantime, don't use that hand for anything. It needs to heal. It's broken."

Hearing that, Flo immediately thought, the wedding photos are going to look good with his hand in that state and what looked like a black eye beginning to show itself.

Annie looked up and caught sight of him. She looked at his bandaged hand and swollen eye. It seemed for a moment as though time had stood still. This was what she was used to dealing with when he was a child. Her next thought was, what would the girl's parents think if he turned up this evening looking like this when they were due to come around. Oh! This was all getting too much.

If he was expecting sympathy, he could think again. This time, she'd had enough.

Standing directly in front of him, she showed no interest in his injuries.

"I suppose you're going to tell me it wasn't your fault. I bet you brought this on yourself. You seem to attract trouble. Don't you think we've got enough to deal with at the moment. That girl doesn't know what she's let herself in for with you."

Continuing her onslaught, her temper getting worse, she carried on, her emotions now reaching fever pitch.

"How are you going to keep your job if you can't use that hand? Have you thought of that? With everything to be sorted out at the meeting tonight, you can't even guarantee bringing any money into the house."

Annie's face was now the colour of someone choking to death. She had spat the words out with a venom Flo had never seen before.

John stood there, silent and open mouthed. Was this his loving, forgiving mother? He didn't recognize her. The silence had now become unbearable.

Flo looked around. Where they had been on their own, they were now the centre of attention. Several people had appeared on hearing raised voices. Now she really hated this place.

"Come on, Annie, let's all get home. We can get this sorted out there. Anyway, your Fred will be wondering where you are by now."

She grabbed Annie's arm and pulled her away from John. He, still looking shocked at his mother's rage, quietly followed them out of the hospital.

Standing on the forecourt it only then dawned on them that they had no transport to get home.

They must have looked a sorry trio because the driver of one of the parked ambulances came over.

"Are you alright? You look like you've got the world's troubles on your shoulders."

Flo explained what had happened and that now they had to get the bus home if they could find out where to catch it.

The driver asked, "Where do you live?"

Annie looked at him and sighed. "Francis Road."

At that moment, he received a message that an ambulance was needed as soon as possible in that area of the East End.

Looking at the sorry trio, he said, "You're in luck. If you get in the back of the ambulance, I can drop you off near your street because I've got a casualty to pick up. You've got to get in the back now before anybody sees you or I'm in trouble."

Once out of the car park, the ambulance sped along, the three of them in the back of it wondering what the neighbours were going to think on hearing the ambulance bell nearing Francis Road. If they were seen getting out of the back of it, there would be a lot of explaining to do. No one would forget this.

Fred had just turned into Francis Road and was feeling very pleased that things that had been on his mind all day would now be sorted out with Jim Venables at the meeting this evening. Annie had calmed down and the front room was pristine again. He hoped John would be on time for the meeting. It would create a good impression.

Having been dropped off by the ambulance driver, the three of them made their way around the corner and into Francis Road. Fred caught sight of them and couldn't understand why John was with them. As they got nearer, his worst fears were realized. He'd brought home even more trouble.

"Bloody hell! What's happened now?"

Annie just wanted to get home. She knew that this meeting was being witnessed by anyone looking out for anything unusual happening. The neighbours had all been alerted that something was up when the distant sound of an ambulance bell had been heard. A story was unfolding in their minds that would require an explanation, even though it was nothing to do with them.

Flo reluctantly left them and returned to her own home. She had a lot to tell Mavis. All this made their problem less important.

Once through the front door, Fred marched John into the kitchen. He then turned on him in anger. Almost spitting out his words he showed a side of himself that had not surfaced for years. Never had he released his anger against one of his own sons as he was about to do now.

"Don't tell me this was an accident at work. I'm not a fool. You've got yourself into a fight, that's obvious. You stupid little bugger. Your cocky attitude has got you into trouble before. You never seem to learn. I only hope it wasn't while you were on the site and that the other bloke is all right, whoever he is."

Walking around the table and getting nearer to John, he

continued on, not waiting for an explanation.

"If you've put someone in hospital, we're going to find the police around here. Who was it you thumped?"

Before John could say anything, Fred continued, raising his voice even more than when he had started his tirade.

"What a stupid bugger you are. You won't be able to work for weeks with that hand which I suppose you've busted. What are you going to do for money now? How's this going to look to those people coming around tonight? It's a shame you didn't break your bloody hand before you started messing around with that girl and getting her pregnant."

Annie gasped at that, although she never uttered a word.

Fred looked at John. "I only hope the other bloke hasn't got any brothers or mates who want to settle things with you or you'll be going around with your back to the wall for some time."

John remained silent, his bandaged hand hanging down by his side.

Fred was beginning to calm down with pauses between shouts. Annie was still standing by the fireplace where she had been since they came in. Her thoughts were that the neighbours would be having a good afternoon's entertainment listening to all this. They had probably heard every word through the paper-thin walls.

Not waiting for John to speak, Fred pointed to the clock on the mantelpiece.

"There's three hours before that family come around. You'd better get yourself over to the flat to get tided up. Put some decent clothes on."

It seemed he was never going to stop shouting orders at

John.

Annie was feeling nothing at this point. She wasn't sure what she wanted to do.

Running his fingers through his hair, Fred needed to compose himself and take control of the situation. Looking at Annie, he could see she needed his support.

"Let's get the front room ready for our visitors, love."

He was trying to sound calm.

"We've got plenty of time. We can pull that little table out into the centre of the room so that you can bring in your nice tea set. We can then, all of us, have a chat about what's best to do about the wedding. I've got a bottle of sherry in the sideboard, if you ladies want a drink, and I can get a few bottles of beer in if the girl's father would like one. He seemed like a bloke who would."

Annie was thinking, this was not the way she'd imagined planning a wedding for one of the boys. Their two younger boys, although now teenagers, weren't anywhere near as much trouble. They were both working and would be in soon. They'd probably know what had happened anyway because news travelled fast in this area.

Back in her own home, Flo was bringing Mavis up to date with everything.

"You know it's times like this that makes you wonder where you went wrong. You do everything you can to bring them up decent and then, what happens, they let you down. The problem Annie and Fred have got to get sorted out is nothing compared to what we've got on our plate."

She paused for a few seconds, giving Mavis no time to respond.

"We don't even know where Beryl is. You do realize that, don't you? If that bloke she's shacked up with demands favours for taking her on as a model, we could be faced with the same problem Annie and Fred have got."

Mavis seemed startled at that.

"Surely, you don't think she'd let him interfere with her, do you? She's supposed to be with him to learn how to be a model."

Flo sighed and looked at Mavis as though she was hearing the words of a nun who believed in the goodness of a saint.

"Mavis, that bloke has probably made the same promise he did to Beryl to loads of other girls. I wonder where they are now. Probably left with memories of his treatment of them and not much else, hopefully. There'll always be blokes like him about."

Mavis looked about to burst into tears. Flo, with her usual answer to everything, said, "Let's put the kettle on and do a bit of tea. We'll both feel better then. I might, in the morning, go to see Annie to find out how the meeting went."

Annie was, once again, standing in front of the dressing table mirror. Her colourful best frock looked nice. She remembered the gold necklace the girl's mother had on and felt disappointed she had no gold jewellery herself. Never mind, this meeting wasn't about her, it was about the future of John, whatever that may hold.

Fred was standing alone in the scullery. He was going over everything on his mind. Thank God his other two sons, Roger and Ken, were not causing any trouble, even though they were teenagers. They seemed to take after their mother and chose to look before they considered leaping, whatever the situation.

His next thought was, where were John and this girl going to live once they were married? They certainly couldn't move in here. The flat John shared with Harry was out of bounds too because Harry had told him that he could bugger off when John suggested the girl could move in with them until they found a place of their own.

As Harry had pointed out, he'd made his bed, quite literally, and now he could lie in it, wherever that may be.

Fred wondered if they could move in with her parents to start with. His thoughts were going from one problem to another.

Leaning against the sink, he looked around the tiny scullery. It wasn't anything special. The landlord hadn't spent any money improving these properties. On the other hand, that was probably a good thing because if he did carry out any repairs, he'd probably put the rent up, and Fred was painfully aware that he had no spare cash. He'd always wanted Annie to stay home to look after the kids and so he was the only one bringing in a wage once Harry and John had moved out.

In the silence of the scullery, his next thought went to how much the wedding was going to cost. He couldn't expect this Jim Venables to pay for it all. It wasn't his fault they were in this position, or was it? After all, his daughter had agreed to let this happen. Perhaps she wasn't as innocent as he made out.

He hadn't noticed that Annie had come downstairs. He looked at her standing by the table in the kitchen. She looked very nice and seemed calm.

The silence was broken as the key turned in the front door lock and that meant John had arrived. Fred glanced at the clock. It was half past six. There was half an hour before the girl and her family were due to arrive.

As he came into the kitchen John, actually looked very smart. He had put on a decent shirt and some trousers which had a crease in them. Wonders would never cease.

The bandaged hand and the fast blackening area around his eye spoilt the image. How was he going to explain those to Jim Venables?

John looked at his mother.

"When are they due to come around? Have I got time to go for a swift half?"

Fred didn't give Annie a chance to answer him.

"No, you bloody haven't. That's all we want. You smelling of beer."

The tension in the room was mounting.

Fred went over to where John was standing.

"What plans have you got to deal with all this? Are you going to chip in with some money to pay for the wedding because we can't put much in the pot. There's so much to pay for."

John seemed surprised that he would have to cough up cash.

With his usual casual attitude, he said, "Don't worry about it, Dad. The girl's father always pays for her wedding."

Fred was reaching boiling point now. He kept running his fingers through his hair and that was always a bad sign.

Annie had gone into the front room and was looking out onto the street through the net curtains. It wasn't long before the van came down the road. She almost ran into the kitchen.

"They're here."

The next couple of hours seemed unreal. This was only the beginning of their problems.

The girl's name was Christine. She was 18 and worked as a secretary in the office of a local firm. Annie told them that their daughter, Sarah, was living and working as a secretary at the Town Hall in Sidcup, Kent. She was pleased that she could match Sarah's achievements with those of their daughter.

Then the situation started to become reality.

Mrs Venables, Vera, thought it best if she made the arrangements for the wedding dress to be chosen. Christine piped up by announcing she wanted her two best friends to be bridesmaids.

Jim Venables suggested they hire the local British Legion hall for the reception. He could probably arrange this at a cut price because he knew the bloke who hired it out.

Although some food was still rationed, he was sure they could come to some arrangement with the canteen people at the hall.

Then, looking directly at Fred, he said, "How many on your side are likely to want to attend? We've made a list and there will be 16 of us."

Annie and Fred were both trying to come to terms with what was happening. They hadn't thought how many people would want to come, apart from immediate neighbours. Annie had thought the wedding tea could have been at their house. The front room and kitchen could hold a few people if they had a sort of buffet and not a sit-down meal. Now all that seemed out of the question.

Looking directly at Annie, Vera asked, "Do you know anyone that could take some photos for us? We've got to put an album together."

With Jim Venables seeming to take the lead in all this, Annie had been sitting quietly wringing her hands in her lap, hoping no one would notice her anxiety. She wanted to stop the pace of all these arrangements. There was still time to think about all this. How long had John known Christine? Did he really want to marry her or was he just doing the right thing to save face? Marriage would put a stop to the only lifestyle he had known. How would he cope with that?

Neither Jim or Vera had asked about John's injuries, although they did seem a bit surprised at the sight of him when they'd arrived.

Annie now thought she ought to say something about them. She had been mostly quiet while all the arrangements were being sorted out. She had never been part of anything like this. She suddenly found her voice.

"Let's hope John's injuries which he got on the building site will be a lot better when it comes to the photographs."

John looked at her, wondering if he should say anything. It was obvious his mother didn't want the family to know they had been caused by a fight and so he stayed quiet.

After another pot of tea had been drunk by the ladies and a bottle or two of beer had been finished off by the men, the only thing left to be decided was the date of the wedding.

Christine was smiling at John and giving him the impression that she wanted to go outside with him to get away from all this. She was wearing a short skirt and kept crossing her legs and then smoothing the material over her hips. John was taking note.

Vera was next to speak, and she said she would see the

vicar with Christine to sort out when the bans would be read. There was a church not far from where they once lived. They had all agreed on a date.

By the time the meeting was over and everyone had left, Fred and Annie were exhausted. Fred felt as though he had been forced into a financial position he could not meet but he didn't say anything to Annie about his worries.

They both sat in the darkening kitchen, silently wondering how they were going to find the money to pay for their share of it all.

John slouched in the only armchair there. He always sat in that chair when he was in trouble when he lived at home. There was the time he had sold some things for a bloke who ran a black market racket. The bloke obtained the goods and he persuaded some of the local lads to find buyers for the stuff. He then paid them for their help. John had been involved with that. The police got to hear about it. Luckily Fred got in first at the station and had argued John's case that he had been easily led and that got John out of trouble eventually. John had spent time sitting in that armchair trying, in his naïve way, to think where he had gone wrong. He'd earnt some money and even given his mum some of it before she knew how he had come by it.

Another time he had been caught as a passenger in a stolen car. He didn't know it was stolen until the police came around. Once again, his dad had pleaded his innocence and ignorance to the police. That was another weekend he had spent immersed between the loose cushions of that old chair.

Now, he was back again seeking its comfort.

Down the street, Flo was wondering how things had gone. She'd hear all about it tomorrow.

Mavis had decided, in her mind, to come to terms with their situation. Perhaps Beryl would have a change of mind one she'd been away from home for a few days. This was the first time anything like this had happened. She didn't know whether to keep in touch with Mrs Davenport at Woolworths in case Beryl came back and wanted a job there again. She seemed a nice woman and Mavis almost felt sorry for her because she hadn't any children of her own. She wondered what her husband was like. They had stayed married, despite not being able to start a family, and so he must love her. Little did Mavis know at this point but, Mr Davenport was going to be one more shock for her to deal with, although she had never met him.

She looked over at Flo who had dozed off in a very uncomfortable position in the armchair. Her head had lolled to one side. She decided to make something for their tea and hoped the sound of her moving about the room would wake her. It did the trick and, slowly, Flo straightened up.

"I must have dozed off there for a minute. What's the time?"

Busying herself in the scullery, Mavis called out, "It's only us two for tea as George has gone out to meet his mates. That boy spends more time with them than he does with us."

Moving across the room to flick the light on, Flo thought, we should be thankful for that. With the Beryl problem her priority worry, she didn't want anything else to happen. If this boyfriend of hers did take advantage of her, she hoped Beryl would come back home to get it sorted out. The worst thing about anything happening in this street was, that no long how much distance was put between the problem and the solution, the neighbours would never let them forget it.

CHAPTER FIVE

Beryl was beginning to feel very uneasy. She had been prepared to expect changes. She was trying to stay calm. The room they were now all in seemed crowded. Justin was getting impatient. He was standing by the camera, tapping his fingers on the top of it. From where she was sitting on the sofa, she couldn't see into the other room but its door was partly open.

Martine started picking up some of the jars of make-up, first holding them up to the light and then glancing over to Beryl. She felt she was being stared at.

Grace silently beckoned her to come over where the clothes rail was. Calling out to Tom, her voice seeming to echo in the silence that had now descended in the room, she asked, "What do you want her in? Are we going for demure and innocent or do you want Miss Control but coy?"

She smiled a knowing smile.

Beryl stood up.

In a defiant mood, she said, "Why is she choosing what clothes I'm going to wear for my photos? That's not right. None of them are glamorous at all."

Martine and Grace now stood side by side. They both gave Tom a knowing look. They were thinking, this one was a bad choice. She was going to be trouble.

Tom realized Beryl was getting agitated.

Gathering her up in his arms, he looked directly at her.

"You must learn to relax, my little pet. We need to get some photos done today and the girls are only here to help you. I have clients who want to see you and, maybe, if they like your photos, you could get invited to go for a meal with them in a very nice hotel. How about that. If you want to be a successful model, you need to wear the right kind of clothes that make you look your best. You have a wonderful figure and your beautiful hair, when it hangs loosely, makes you look very professional."

Grace was doing her best to think of something to say that would convince Beryl the clothes on the rail were the best ones for the photos. Looking at her, she said, "I think you would look really nice in one of these suits we have on the rail."

She pulled the jacket and skirt out from the rail and held it up.

"You could think of yourself as a sort of secretary. That's a very good job and people will think you are both pretty and clever. With your hair tumbling down onto your shoulders, the white blouse will show your lovely complexion up a treat. You could sit on that tall stool over there and that would also make your legs look good. You have a lot of very nice features."

Before Grace could say any more, Beryl broke away from Tom.

"What is she talking about? The pictures I've seen of models show them wearing lovely dresses and lots of jewellery."

Grabbing her bag, she began sorting through its contents.

"I can show you what I mean. I've got one of my magazines here."

Both Martine and Grace stopped what they were doing

and stared at Beryl as she handed the magazine to Tom.

"Look. This is what I mean."

Justin had been trying to set the camera up and was waiting patiently by the window. He had remained silent while all this was going on. He smiled and wondered how Tom was going to deal with this situation. This was going to be very interesting. There had been a few times in the past when the girls he 'recruited' had seen through his management business. They had found themselves being subjected to threats if they didn't co-operate. He could be nasty if he thought the girls were wasting his precious time. Tom's requests for them to take up certain poses becoming more like an order than a suggestion. So far, though, he had been able to persuade the girls to think of themselves as starlets with great futures ahead of them. This one seemed a bit more of a challenge. He wasn't going to let that interfere with his plans, though. She was younger than most of the others and that would appeal to most of his customers. Fresh to the market, so to speak, and he knew exactly which of his 'people' would pay good money for photos of this one. He felt he was on to a definite winner.

Martine made the gesture of raising her hand to her mouth as though she was having a drink. Tom noticed.

"Look, why don't we all have a drink and talk through the scene. That's what professional people do. You mustn't get yourself in a state or your photos won't look good."

He was still holding the magazine she had handed him. He held it behind his back and walked her over to the small bar in the room.

"We could all have a little drink which will make you more relaxed."

Beryl was not having any of that.

"No. I don't want a drink. I'm not used to that. I'm getting a headache now."

She was taking on the appearance of a naughty child now with her attitude.

Martine stepped forward and put her arm around Beryl's shoulder.

Why don't you take one of my headache pills and then we can both go out to get some fresh air. We could stroll along the high street for a few minutes. That always works for me when I get a headache."

Beryl looked at her for a few seconds.

"Yes. That would be all right."

She was warming to Martine now. She looked at Tom. He was still holding the magazine.

Martine went over to the table the collection of make-up was on and, picking up a small package, took one of the pills out. Handing Beryl a glass of water, she passed the tablet to her. Beryl looked at it.

"This is a funny colour. The headache pills my mum takes are usually white. This one is like the sweets they sell in our corner shop. Are they really for a headache?"

Martine looked over at Justin who was now tapping his wristwatch. Tom and Grace were standing together and silent.

Smiling, Martine said, "They don't take long to work. They are special and are what starlets take in America. You'll feel fine once we've had our little walk."

Beryl looked at her suspiciously. How did she know so much about what they took in America? She hoped, in her innocence, that Martine wasn't just saying that. Perhaps she was seeing a nice side to Martine she didn't know existed.

With one gulp from a glass of water, she swallowed the pill.

Once outside on the street, Beryl slid her arm around Martine's and they strode off. The fresh air was good and it was a nice day. Beryl felt, for the first time since her adventure had begun, that she was lucky Tom had chosen her for this photo shoot, as he called it.

Martine, still clutching Beryl's arm, gently walked her around the next turning. There was a small park which seemed to be taking up one side of the street. The trees were full of leaves which were rustling in the gentle breeze. The hedges were held back by railings and Beryl could see some colourful flower beds. Stopping to look through the railings, she said, "Isn't that pretty? We don't have anything like that where I live now. It reminds me of when I was little."

She was feeling very relaxed now.

There was traffic moving around her but it seemed distant. The flowers in the park seemed to be waving to her in the breeze.

"Has your headache gone?"

Martine was sure Beryl was now ready to return to the salon. Her shoulders seemed more relaxed and she wasn't holding onto Martine's arm now quite so tightly.

Looking at her, Beryl said, "Do you know, I think it has."

She started giggling.

Guiding her around to the way back, Martine said, "Let's get back now or they'll wonder where we are. Justin can take some photos of you in that nice suit and then we can go back to the flat so that you can rest."

Beryl looked at her as they swung around to return.

"I feel much better now. I ought to do what Tom wants because he knows lots about models and starlets."

Martine hid a smile.

Guiding her back up the steep flight of stairs, Martine thought, if that's what one 'headache pill' does for her, anything could happen.

Tom and Grace were waiting for them and Justin breathed a sigh of relief. Perhaps now they could get on with it.

The girls sat Beryl down and began applying some of the make-up from the tubs strewn across the table. The whole time they were talking to her and telling her how fantastic she was going to look. The make-up smelt wonderful as they patted it over her cheeks and swept a very soft brush around her hairline. She had to sit very still while they traced a line over her eyelids and applied mascara to her lashes. She wanted to laugh about it but knew she had to stay very still. They patted what they called 'blush' across her cheeks and finally, a small brush was used to apply some lipstick. She had never seen that done before. Her mum would never have used a brush for that. If she used lipstick at all, she just wiped it across her lips.

The girls stood back and admired their work. There was no doubt about it, Beryl was a very pretty girl indeed.

It was now a couple of hours since Beryl had taken the headache pill and Tom had wondered if they could persuade her to take another one. Justin hoped, by now, Beryl would be ready to get into the clothes that had been chosen for her so that the photos could be taken. He knew exactly what he was supposed to do, and the afternoon was racing away. He would have to use all his skills to get the lighting right.

Tom stood by Beryl as she looked at her image in the mirror. She had been transformed into what her gran would call a 'glamour girl' and she liked it.

Tom looked at her and said, "I told you the girls were here to help you look like a model, didn't I. It's time to get you dressed and ready for the photos."

That brought Beryl back to reality.

"I can get myself dressed if you don't mind."

Before she could say any more, Martine said, "You don't want to give yourself another headache, do you, so why don't you have another of my little pills. The last one relaxed you, didn't it?"

Beryl sighed. She had to agree that it did.

"All right, then, if you think it will help me. I'll have another one."

After carefully sidelining Beryl, they managed to get her dressed as they wanted her to look and that look was dominant and a little risqué.

Posing and pouting for the camera, the blouse being left open to reveal part of Beryl's breast and the skirt arranged to show most of her thigh, the photos would give the impression that this young lady would be a lot of fun to know. They were all talking to her the whole time Justin was taking the shots.

Beryl was giggling a lot now as the second pill took effect and Justin was working as fast as he could before she calmed down. She seemed totally unaware of what was going on around her. This was a nice feeling. She couldn't understand what was happening but, then, she didn't care. She remembered back to the time her friend had given her some sherry to drink as a dare. It was very sweet and, by the time she'd finished it, the feeling of being relaxed made her laugh.

Justin was very pleased with the way she was posing because he kept saying so.

When the girls told her there was a dress she could put on which was very special, Beryl felt very important.

She giggled when she couldn't find which was the back of it or the front. It was very lacey and didn't seem to have any buttons. She thought it was very feminine and liked how it felt next to her skin. She looked at herself in the mirror that stood against the wall. She finally felt like a starlet. She couldn't let go of the feeling she was dreaming all this. She kept blinking, thinking she was going to wake up.

With lots of lights shining out from the adjoining room, Beryl wondered what was in there. She was sure she could see flashes of light but what could they be?

Tom saw her looking towards the door.

"That room is very special. I don't let all the models use it. Do you want to have a look?"

Once more, looking again at her reflection in the mirror, Beryl was excited at how nice she looked. For some reason, she wanted to walk around feeling the dress floating along with her.

"Yes, I'd like to see what's in there."

She was now feeling very adventurous. Normally, she would have shied away from anything she was not sure of, but she felt so relaxed that the bright lights in front of her could only mean that something good was in that room. They were drawing her like a moth to a flame. Her thoughts were racing with imagination. Perhaps it would be like a film studio behind the door. Tom would probably know about them. Perhaps, as the photos Justin had taken of her were so good, this was going to be a screen test. Tom probably knew all about those as well. She couldn't stop smiling. She felt so pleased with herself. She wanted to twirl around so that the dress could follow her movements and gently come to a stop around her body. Raising her hand to her lips, she blew kisses to Martine and Grace. She wondered for a moment why she had done that but then she felt so happy. Although they were only a few feet away from her, the room seemed bigger than before.

With her confidence increasing, she looked at Tom and said, "Well, if you're going to show me what's in your secret room, should Martine and Grace still be here?

Without saying anything, Tom took hold of her arm and guided her into the room. He knew it was just a bedroom. The large bed had silk sheets across it with a bedhead which was, in Beryl's eyes, quite luxurious and made of her favourite material, velvet. There were lots of silk cushions scattered about and she couldn't understand, in her confused state, why anyone would want them all there.

How lucky she was that she had met Tom.

With every step she took in the room, there were beautiful colours. She wanted to just stand still and take it all in, but she couldn't. There seemed to be a rainbow in the room. It reminded her of a kaleidoscope she used to have where the colours kept changing when she moved it. She began walking around the bed. How pretty it looked with the silk cushions seeming to shine. She giggled and, looking at Tom, wanted him to take her in his arms. That always made her feel special. She felt quite lightheaded and, as her hair had tumbled over her face, she raised her hand and ran her fingers through it. It felt very soft which she hadn't noticed before.

Tom was observing her from a distance. He wasn't sure if her reaction to the pills was good or not. She seemed to be searching for something as she twisted and turned around the room, like a dancer. She noticed some pretty curtains at the window and they seemed to be moving, but how could that be? The window was closed. Tom thought he ought to take control here.

Justin had moved into the room and was, once again, setting the camera up. Martine and Grace were standing in the doorway observing all this.

Picking up a teddy bear which had been left on a shelf, Tom handed it to Beryl. She instinctively cuddled it.

Suddenly, she lost her balance and landed on the bed, giggling. Tom rushed forward.

"Be careful, my little pet. You could have hurt yourself."

Gazing up into his eyes, Beryl hoped he was going to kiss her but, instead, he stood back. His mind was working out how he could use this scenario for a photo. Beryl was ready for the next pose, he was sure.

Her milky white legs were now dangling over the side of the bed. Tom knew this was a chance he couldn't waste.

Leaning over, he pulled her up and sat on the bed next to her.

"If I stand over there with Justin, you could blow a kiss to the camera. That would make a very nice photo. You could also slip your dress down and hold some of those lovely cushions in front of you and peek over the top of them."

Justin was smiling but silent. Tom certainly knew how to persuade these girls to do what he wanted. The customers he would sell the photos to would pay good money for them. He'd only slipped up once when he went too far on one of these sessions and had persuaded two of the girls to take part in a near naked romp on the bed. Those photos had been sold a few times and had come to the attention of the police. He was lucky on that occasion that he hadn't been charged with soliciting girls for immoral earnings. The girls in question had told the police that the photos taken were at a private party and they had agreed to them. This girl, he thought, was acting as though she was drunk.

Time was running out and he knew that the pills would soon leave her wanting to sleep. Before he could let that happen, there was one last photo he hoped to get.

Scooping her up in his arms from the bed, he held her tightly.

"Would you like to wear a very special swimming costume? I have got one that is the same as the one Betty Grable wears in her films and you know how beautiful she is. It would look perfect on you."

Beryl was now feeling almost giddy with excitement.

Looking at him, she said, "Oh, yes, please, Tom."

He pulled her closer and said, "There is a screen over there where you can take off your dress and put the swimming costume on. The mirror on the wall will show you how great you look."

Almost staggering now, Beryl reached the screen and found the dress she was wearing had slipped from her slender body and had landed on the floor. Standing almost naked in front of the mirror, she didn't notice Justin had been taking photos of her. The outline of her pert young breasts, slender hips and the almost teasing pubic hair could just be seen underneath the scanty knickers she was wearing. Slipping them off, the full beauty of her young body was revealed.

Justin could see Tom observing both Beryl and himself as he was becoming aroused. Before Beryl realized what was happening, Justin stepped from behind the camera and drew Beryl's lips to his. With closed eyes, she responded to his touch as his fingers explored the teasing area between her legs which were slightly apart now. She didn't seem to be resisting. His touch felt gentle and she liked the way he was making her feel. His lips had now reached her breast and she could feel him sucking on her nipple. She couldn't understand why she was not objecting. It felt so good.

Opening her eyes, she caught her reflection in the mirror and could see Justin kneeling in front of her, his face only inches from the top of her legs. She could feel his fingers exploring and pressing gently on the soft wet tissue between her legs, making her gasp with excitement.

The mirror image in front of her suddenly brought her to her senses. She stood back. What was happening? Tom was now behind the camera and had been taking all the shots he could only have hoped for.

Justin was still kneeling on the floor. He suddenly got up and rushed out of the room.

Beryl felt a wave of tiredness overwhelm her and she felt she was going to collapse.

Martine and Grace appeared before she fell and guided her into the other room. They realized the pills she had been given were having a strange effect on her. It was decided they would dress her and take her back to the flat. Perhaps she just needed to sleep.

Tom's thoughts were now racing. He knew several of his clients would pay anything he asked for a set of the photos that had just been taken. This had been the best session ever. The first name which sprang to mind was Arthur Davenport. He appreciated the photos Tom had come up with in the past, but these were dynamite.

"Tom. We'd better get her back to the flat as soon as possible. She needs to sleep this off."

Grace was standing over Beryl with a worried look on her face. In the past, the girls they'd used for these photos were usually no problem. They'd sometimes agreed to take a pill to relax them and it had worked.

"Perhaps we shouldn't have given her two of those bloody things. Now we'll have to make sure she comes out of the stupor she seems to be in. Give me a hand here. I can't get her dressed and down the stairs into the car on my own."

It seemed to take a while to drag Beryl to her feet. She was silent and not very responsive. Suddenly she laughed out loud and then collapsed again onto the chair they had only just raised her from.

Justin emerged from the other room and sheepishly came to help.

"If you get her back to the flat, that will leave me here to develop the film in peace. How many do you want of them?"

Tom was already making a mental note of his best customers and totting up what he could get from them.

"You'd better make it four copies. If you can do them by tomorrow when I call in, I can probably shift them in a couple of hours."

Martine was now standing at the foot of the stairs with the door wide open. Grace and Tom were supporting the still unstable Beryl down the stairs, trying to prevent her from banging her shins against the wall. She was like a limp rag doll. Her head hung down but she was talking all the time. None of it made any sense. Every few steps taken made her laugh out loud.

Once in the back of the car, the girls sat either side of her to stop her falling forward. This had become a nightmare.

Back at the flat, Beryl was laid on her side on the bed, still fully clothed. Tom placed a pillow behind her so that she couldn't roll onto her back. They all quietly left the room.

The evening was spent with the girls checking on Beryl every now and again. They all finally went to bed around midnight.

Grace was first up the next morning. She liked the peace sitting on her own for a while before the day unveiled its surprises and there were usually a few. Things has been going well for them. They seemed to be a good team. It never failed to surprise her that some of Tom's customers, being respectable married men, were always only too ready to spend their hard-earned cash on pornographic photos. If only their wives knew. Still, there was no harm done.

The flat was quiet. The only noise she could hear was coming from the adjoining flats.

She'd just finish the cup of tea she'd made herself and then she would check on Beryl. I wonder, she thought, if Tom would use her again as she had been such a nuisance to work with. His other girls came and went as they pleased. When they were short of cash, they always contacted Tom who put some work their way. One of his best customers was Arthur Davenport. He was always willing to pay cash for the photos and sometimes took his favourite girl to a hotel for a weekend, telling his wife he was on a business trip.

Her thoughts were interrupted when Tom emerged from his bedroom already dressed and holding the notebook which was what he called his 'Bible'. In that he had all the contact numbers and names that he had used in the past.

"Is she up yet?"

Grace shook her head.

Tom was hoping Beryl would be able to help the girls with a few errands he wanted them to run.

"I'm not having her staying in bed all morning. She might think that's what models or starlets do, but she has got a rude awakening coming. You'd better wake her up."

Putting her cup down, Grace was annoyed her few minutes of silence had been broken. She went into the bedroom that used to be Jane's before she left. The only sound she could hear from Beryl was a deep breath being taken and then, after what seemed to be a long pause, she heard a gasping sound.

Approaching the bed, it seemed that Beryl had moved down the bed and was now lying with her legs pulled up as if in cramp. There was a dried saliva trail which ran from the corner of her mouth. Her lips seemed to have lost their colour and were now slightly parted, revealing what looked like blood from her tongue which she must have bitten.

In a blind panic, Grace shouted out to Tom.

"Quick. Get in here now. Something's not right."

In seconds, he was standing by the bed.

"Christ! What's happened here? Is she still breathing? Tell me she's still breathing."

Hearing the blind panic in their voices, Martine appeared in the doorway.

"What's going on?"

Tom was leaning over Beryl.

"Do either of you know what to do?"

Grace was beginning to panic now. Her heart was thumping and she was feeling short of breath. Her eyes were darting from side to side looking at the way Beryl was laying on the bed.

"We've got to get her out of here. She looks awful. Should we take her to the hospital? They'll know what to do."

Tom was getting worried now. If they took her to hospital, they'd know she'd taken some sort of drug.

Without any more hesitation, his only thought was to get her out of the flat somehow.

"We can't keep her here and we can't take her home."

With rising panic in his voice, he said, "Get her bag and see if there's a diary or something in there with the name and address of a friend we could contact."

Martine grabbed Beryl's bag. Among all the usual things a girl carried around, she was relieved to find what looked like an address book. Pulling it out and flicking through the pages, she said, "She's got a note in here with the name of someone called Ann. That might be one of her friends. She may be able to help. There's no phone number but there's an address. It looks like a local factory address. That must be where she works. One of us could go around there and ask if Beryl could stay with her wherever she lives. It would only be for a day or two."

Still looking at Beryl in her stupor, Tom was beginning to think those bloody photos had better sell well or I'll be right pissed off.

He'd had enough of this.

"One of you had better get around to that factory sharpish and see if you can make arrangements for her to stay with this friend."

Grace decided she'd go. She didn't particularly like Beryl but she didn't want any harm to come to her.

"Martine, you clean her up a bit while I'm gone."

That turned out to be no simple task. Beryl had wet herself during the night.

Martine carefully wiped her face and brushed Beryl's hair. Beryl did not respond. She then, after a struggle, put some dry knickers on her. The skirt she was wearing would have to stay on though. Her clothes were badly creased, showing they had been slept in.

Beryl was still not responding.

This had never happened before with any of their other girls who had taken one of Tom's pills. She hoped Beryl would wake up and everything would be back to normal, although in the pit of her stomach, she didn't think that would be the case. What if they couldn't bring her round? They couldn't get her to drink some coffee or something. They would have trouble even sitting her up. She didn't just seem to be asleep. She seemed to be unconscious.

Tom had left the flat.

Grace wrote down the address from the diary and decided it would be a bus ride to get there. She didn't like travelling on buses. She'd got used to being in Tom's car. She roughly knew where the factory would be. Sitting on the jolting bus, she had forgotten the smell of the people close by. The sun streaming in through the grimy windows made the journey more pungent. Finally, the bus came to a halt at the stop she wanted. She almost leapt from the small platform at the back of it in an effort to take in some fresh air.

Which way should she go? She didn't want to waste time looking for the factory and so stopped a woman passing by who was carrying some shopping. She must be local.

Producing the written address, Grace asked if she knew where the place was.

Putting her shopping bags down, the woman read the address.

"That's not a factory, dear. That place is only a couple of rooms in the back of that building over there."

She was pointing to a grimy looking alleyway opposite.

"They make curtains and stuff. If you're looking for work, I don't think they're taking any more people just now. I could be wrong though."

Grace was appalled that the woman would think she was looking for work in a place like that. This bloody Beryl was causing more trouble than she liked. This is not like it should be.

She was here now. She made her way along the alleyway between the buildings and various waste bins and found the door with a company name on it. She knocked. Nothing happened. She pushed on the door which immediately opened. The noise of all the sewing machines was obviously why her feeble little knock on the door couldn't be heard.

She stood there, not knowing what to do. She'd never been anywhere like this before. The girls all continued, heads down, fingers pressing and guiding material through the machines in an unending motion of twisting and turning.

A tall woman appeared from nowhere.

"Can I help you?"

Her tone was clipped and urgent. Grace almost felt threatened as though she had entered a domain foreign to anything she had known before.

Looking directly at the woman, she almost spluttered, "Can I to speak to a girl called Ann? I think she works here."

The woman arched her back and drew in a deep breath.

"I've already had someone here asking to speak to her and I'm not going to put up with her getting any more visitors. She is here to work. Now please leave."

Grace was taken aback by this and wanted to turn and leave but that wouldn't solve their problem. She had got to speak to the girl.

"Does she have a tea break? I need to speak to her then."

The woman was getting less patient now.

"You can do all the talking you want once she has finished work and that won't be for another two hours. Until then, I suggest you go away and wait for her to leave the premises. Now please go."

Grace did not like this woman. Her voice seemed to have become embedded in her mind. Two hours! What should she do for that long in this awful part of town? She had no choice but to find somewhere to go. She looked at her wrist watch. It was 3 o'clock. That meant she wouldn't be able to speak to this Ann until 5.

On her way here, she remembered seeing a big official

looking building with the word 'library' on the front. Perhaps she could wait in there. She hadn't been in a library for years.

Making her way along the street, Grace realized that the short distance she had travelled on the bus was, really, not far from the area where she lived and yet it all seemed foreign to her.

She reached the library building. Looking up at its façade it almost seemed ominous. It reminded her a bit of school. She went in. It felt surprisingly welcome.

She automatically looked up at the balcony encircling the ceiling which seemed to wrap itself around the building. Shelves of books were nestled in wooden panels waiting to be plucked out and investigated. Ahead of her, people were silently concentrating on volumes chosen for a reason. No one registered or noticed her presence. She sat down on a bench with the nervousness of a child alone. In this silent arena, she felt the tangle of atmospheric surprise and security. Still no one had approached her.

Turning her head, she found that the area she had unwittingly found sanctuary in had books along its shelves relating to some of the world's famous artists. She reached out and pulled a large volume from the shelf which showed the works of landscape painters.

Turning the pages, she discovered wonderful gardens, beautiful lakes and magical forests. Could those places really exist, she wondered.

Eager to find more, she stretched her hand out and found a thick volume showing a very grand house on its cover. Sliding it onto her lap she slowly opened it up, wanting to be surprised and amazed. The pages felt silky and smooth.

The grand houses in front of her were from another age and had such beautiful interiors that she could only imagine what it must have been like to exist in such settings.

Eagerly turning page after page, she started to feel disappointment at her own existence.

She slowly closed the book.

What was she doing with her life? She suddenly felt the trap of its isolation.

Looking up, she noticed the library had posted famous quotes along a section of shelving. She read the one nearest to her.

'It's never too late to be what you might have been.' Eleanor Roosevelt.

CHAPTER SIX

Grace reluctantly left the library. She had to get back to that awful alleyway in time for the girls leaving the place. She didn't know who Ann was or what she looked like.

Waiting for the girls to spill out of the building, the only way she was going to attract Ann's attention was to call out her name. With the noise of the passing traffic and the rising chatter of the girls, Grace simply yelled out 'Ann'. Two of the girls looked over at her. One of them came up to her.

"What do you want? I don't think I know you."

Grace stepped forward.

"I'm looking for a girl called Ann who has a friend called Beryl. I must speak to her urgently."

The girl turned her head away.

"That's her over there."

She was pointing to a small very petite girl who looked about the same age as Beryl.

The girl was watching what was going on as the rest of the crowd began dispersing out of the alley.

Shouting over the noise of the traffic and chatter, she called out, "There's someone over here that wants a word."

Threading her way through the other girls, she reached Grace.

"Can I help you?"

She didn't know whether to dread what this woman was

going to say or not.

Without hesitating, Grace asked if she knew someone called Beryl. The girl immediately felt afraid of what she was going to tell her.

"Yes. She's my best friend. Is she all right?"

Pulling her to one side of the alley, Grace didn't want to alarm her about the situation, but she did want to resolve it.

Smiling, she told her, "Beryl is not feeling very well but doesn't want to go home and worry her mum. She wondered if she could stay with you for a day or two."

The girl looked startled.

"What's the matter with her then?"

Grace was trying to keep her voice on a level which sounded normal but also concerned for Beryl.

Smiling, she said, "I expect you have some days when you don't want to worry your mum if you don't feel right. I'm sure you know what I mean. Beryl only wants to have about a day to stay in bed and have a sleep without bothering anyone."

The girl was now wondering what she should do. She bit on her bottom lip and frowned.

"Well. If she isn't well, I suppose she could stay at my house because it just so happens my mum is away for two days visiting her sick sister. I don't suppose she would mind Beryl sleeping at ours for a night. She used to do that sometimes when we were little."

Grace couldn't believe she was hearing this. It was the answer to her prayers.

"What do you want me to do then?" the girl asked.

Before Grace could answer, she said, "Tell Beryl to come around to mine. I'll be home in about half an hour. She knows where I live."

Immediately Grace wondered how she was going to explain that Beryl was only semi-conscious. She didn't want to alarm the girl.

"Let's walk on a bit."

The others had all dispersed now.

"I don't want to be a nuisance, but I think the best thing would be for me to bring her around to your place if you could give me your address."

It was obvious the girl was becoming wary now. Grace had to keep her attention.

"Why don't you go home and I can bring Beryl around to you in about an hour. That would be best wouldn't it?"

The girl seemed to want to help her friend and agreed. She wrote down her address and handed it to Grace.

They parted with Grace looking for a bus stop where she could get the bus to return her to the flat.

Both Martine and Tom were waiting for her. They had managed to get Beryl to a chair where she remained slumped. Her general appearance was still causing them concern. She felt very cold to the touch and was completely unresponsive. Her eyes were closed as though she was sleeping but her mouth remained open causing a slight trickle of saliva to pass over her lower lip.

Grace told them what had been agreed and the other two visibly relaxed a little. Martine took Beryl's bag and coat while Tom and Grace supported and half carried Beryl down the stairs wondering if she knew she was leaving the flat. They were not sure if she knew what was happening. There had been a slight response from her when they told her that they were taking her to Ann's house so that she could rest for a while.

The journey to Ann's house was a nightmare. Beryl seemed to be going in and out of reality in her own mind. One minute she was silent and the next she wanted to stand up and dance. Both Grace and Martine were holding her down in the back of the car. It seemed a long time before they reached the address on the slip of paper Ann had given them.

On seeing the car draw up, Ann, who had been looking out of the window, came rushing to the front door, smiling and happy to see her friend.

She stood on the pavement and watched them part drag and part hold up Beryl getting her out of the car.

Anxiously, Ann walked forward towards the car. Both Grace and Martine had a strange look on their faces. It was not a smile or a frown. They had to keep up the pretence that Beryl was simply not feeling too well.

"How are you, Beryl?"

Ann was trying to understand what she was witnessing. Beryl didn't seem just not well, but drugged. What she was seeing was frightening. Her friend seemed unable to speak.

Beryl's usually glorious silky hair, which she was very proud of, was hanging limply and knotted down the side of her face, some of it seeming to be stuck by sweat to her cheeks. What make-up Ann could see was smeared and looked hideous.

Pushing passed her, Grace and Martine walked towards the front door of Ann's home supporting Beryl whose feet were dragging along the pavement.

Once inside the house, they settled Beryl onto a settee just inside the first room they came to. She crumpled into a slump.

Martine left Beryl's bag on the floor and both girls left with the advice that Beryl simply needed to sleep.

It wasn't long before Ann realized something was seriously wrong. Beryl's breathing was so loud and erratic that Ann wondered, after every breath exhaled, would she take another.

Beryl had not moved or responded to Ann's questions. Also, her general appearance was dreadful. What had happened to her? Her clothes were also disheveled. She didn't know what to do.

A knock on the front door brought her out of her anguished thoughts.

Almost stumbling along the small passage, she wondered who it could be. Pulling open the door, it was the tall figure of Cyril, one of her neighbours. She had known him for most of her life although her only real contact with him had been saying hello to him if they met in the street. Her mother, of course, knew him very well. He had a worried look on his face.

"It's Ann, isn't it? You know who I am, of course. I wondered if you were all right. Your mum told me her sister wasn't feeling too good and that she was going to see her for a day or two. I think she wanted me to just keep an eye out for you."

Ann was silent for a few seconds and then opened the door fully. Before she could say anything, Cyril peered around her and into the passage.

"I saw a car arrive and some people were helping a friend of yours into your home. Please don't think I'm being nosey, but your friend did look as though she was drunk. She didn't seem to be able to stand up. Is she all right? Does she need any help?"

Ann didn't know whether to be pleased he had seen Beryl's arrival and the state she was in or whether he would be able to tell what was wrong with her if she let him come in. She knew that, in the past, he had been an orderly at the hospital for many years. Perhaps her could tell her how to sober Beryl up or something. She knew people were sick if they were drunk and she didn't want that to happen.

Standing away from the door, she said, "You had better come in. My friend isn't very well and I'm not sure what's wrong with her."

Beryl had been left on the settee in Ann's front room. It was what her mum called her 'best' room. They only used it for special occasions. Other than that, they spent their time in the kitchen.

She guided Cyril to where Beryl was, part sitting, part slouched.

Cyril stood back and looked at her.

"Has she spoken to you since she arrived?"

Ann shook her head.

He went close to Beryl and bending down, gently lifted her chin up so that he could see her face. Her eyes remained closed. He noticed her erratic breathing and the sweat now breaking out along her forehead. Placing her limp hand in his, it felt very cold. It was obvious to him that this girl needed help and he didn't think she was drunk.

Ann was now standing a few feet away, not wanting anything to do with this situation. She was feeling scared now.

Cyril turned to her and had already decided the girl needed to be taken to hospital.

"I've got a car and we could both take her to hospital. I don't know what's wrong with her but I think it would be best if a doctor could see her. Can you contact her parents? They could perhaps meet us there."

Ann was getting really scared now. They didn't have a telephone and neither did Beryl's mum and nan. She'd have to go around to their house to see them.

"She lives with her mum and nan. She doesn't have a dad. I would have to go to their house to tell them what's going on."

Cyril could see Ann was becoming tearful.

"I tell you what. You tell me where they live and I'll get my wife to go around there to let them know we've taken her to hospital because she's not well."

As confused as Ann was, she thought that was a good idea.

What seemed like hours later, Ann was sitting on a metal bench in a sterile corridor which seemed to stretch forever. There were no tables, no chairs, just metal benches. The walls were painted white and there were some notice boards at what seemed like regular intervals along the walls. Typed-up sheets of paper were pinned to them in an anonymous way. Did anyone ever read what was written on them?

There were other people sitting along this corridor and all of them were silent and distant. It was as if they were all waiting for terrible news.

She didn't know where Beryl was. Cyril had spoken to the person on reception when they arrived and had accompanied Beryl with a nurse to a doorway at the end of the corridor. Perhaps that was where the doctor was. She hadn't been brought out again. She'd never been in a hospital before and didn't like being here now.

Ann was dreading Beryl's mum and nan arriving. They would be as confused as she was. What could she tell them? Who were those people that brought Beryl to her door? Why didn't they say what had happened to her? Why didn't they wait to make sure she was all right?

The double doors at the entrance to the corridor swung open and there they were.

The next few minutes were spent in conversational turmoil. Questions kept coming but the answers were no more than a tangle of confusion and expectation.

Beryl's nan decided to get some answers herself.

Before she reached the room where Beryl had been taken, Cyril emerged. Not knowing who he was, Beryl's nan immediately assumed he was someone who worked there. They almost collided.

Looking directly at him, she said, "I'm here with my daughter, Mavis Taylor, and it's her girl that's been brought in. Can you tell us what's going on?"

Looking along the corridor, he could see Ann talking to a woman he assumed to be Beryl's mother.

"I'm a neighbour of Ann and was there when your granddaughter was taken to her house. She didn't look well and I decided she should have a doctor see her. Someone will come out to speak to you in a minute. They will be able to answer your questions. The only thing I know is that they think she has taken some drugs."

Flo put her hand up to her mouth and gasped.

"But she hasn't been to see the doctor for a long time. She hasn't got any drugs. No. That can't be right."

Cyril realized she didn't understand.

"No, I don't mean medicine. She might have taken some drugs that young people use at parties now. It makes them feel good."

The scene being acted out in this foreign place was unreal. Cyril was witnessing the distress and disbelief of Beryl's nan and mother who were trying to, not only come to terms with the fact that Beryl was in hospital, but also that she must have been mixing with some nasty people. They had nearly poisoned her. That's the only way Mavis could see it. Had they done it deliberately? Her daughter had been naïve and had trusted them. Who were these people?

At the flat, Grace and Martine were wondering how Beryl's friend was coping. Had they done the right thing? All Tom wanted was for the girl to be offloaded and as far away from him and the flat as possible. His attitude surprised them both.

Grace hadn't mentioned her time spent in the library. In her, oh so public life, she wanted to keep something secret. She thought the others wouldn't understand the impact that library visit had made on her. She felt safe, calm and pleasantly happy while she was there.

Before she had left, she noticed some bookmarks scattered on a table. They were left there for people to use. She had wanted something to remember her visit by and had picked one up and put it in her bag. It must still be there. Yes. She found it.

On one side of it was a floral print and on the other were some quotations. She began to read them.

'The only experiences you regret are the ones you've

never had.'

'One of the nice things about problems is that a good many of them do not exist except in our imagination.'

'Anonymous friendships are the ones we remember.'

She stopped reading them. Anonymous friendships.

That would sum up her experience of knowing Beryl. Whatever the outcome of this incident with her was, she would never forget her.

They didn't mean to get her in that state. She'd just had a bad reaction to the pills. She'd be all right in a day or two. Her thoughts were confused now. She'd never get used to the way Tom exploited these girls. She was beginning to get a conscience.

The next morning, Justin, having got the photos printed for an impatient Tom, had to admit they were good.

Tom was trawling through his 'Bible' to see which of his customers would be in their usual lunchtime watering hole so that he could catch them at the right time. His first thoughts went to Arthur Davenport. Yes, he decided, he would be the first customer to see them. He never quibbled about the price.

Both Grace and Martine were quietly glad that yesterday was over.

Tom's mind was focused on finding Arthur Davenport this lunchtime. Arthur's routine never changed. He would be in The Red Lion at 1 o'clock, that was for sure. Tom headed straight over there.

The familiar buzz of the place and the smell of the beer was almost comforting. A heavy swell of cigarette smoke seemed to drift backwards and forwards above the heads of the customers like a polluted tide that had left its mark on the ceiling and the walls.

Tom's gaze pierced through the throng of drinkers, each silently acknowledging an unspoken friendship. He couldn't see Arthur. He was always in here at this hour. Perhaps he was just late today.

Going over to the bar, he ordered a G and T and a pint of best bitter. He took them over to a table by the door. As he put them down on the marble table top, the door flung open and Arthur walked in.

He didn't see Tom at first but then, scanning the place, he realized he was only feet away from him.

"What are you doing in here today? It's all right for some. I've just had my customer area increased which has meant I've got more people to deal with now."

Tom smiled.

"Well, I've got a nice surprise for you that will improve your day."

Pointing to the beer on the table he looked at him. "I've got one in for you."

Arthur sat down.

Tom reached into the inside pocket of his jacket and pulled out the photos. He surreptitiously passed them to Arthur under the table.

There was silence between them in this cacophony of sound as he looked at them. He was speechless. He then looked at Tom and smiled.

"How much?"

The rest of the meeting passed swiftly and, in no time at all, money had been handed over and the pals parted.

Tom was, once again, scanning the contacts in his 'Bible'

to distribute more snaps.

A day after Beryl had been admitted to hospital, the doctor decided it was safe for her to be taken home. After trying to explain to Mavis and Flo that the substance found in her blood test appeared to be one of the many drugs which had come over from America and which were making their way into the London party scene, Beryl would suffer no lasting damage and, having come out of the deep sleep she was in, seemed more embarrassed than anything else.

Mavis had calmed down and Flo had decided that this was another lesson learned. Having a teenage girl in the house was going to be a bit of a trial from now on. Things were changing. She was just glad that Beryl had a friend like Ann who had looked out for her. Even possibly saved her life.

Once home, Mavis tried to act as though nothing had changed. She hoped Beryl would go back to being her old self. Perhaps if, after a few days, Beryl might want to get her old job back. Mavis wondered if she might go to Woolworths and have a word with Mrs Davenport. She seemed an understanding woman even though she didn't have any children herself. Yes. That's what she would do. She'd wait a few days and then go to see her. Mavis realized then that she didn't know the woman's name. She wouldn't say anything to Beryl just now though.

Elaine and Arthur Davenport lived in a large house on the outskirts of Wanstead, an area of London which seemed to be colonized by couples where the husband was in business and the wife stayed home. However, Elaine Davenport was an educated woman who liked the fact that she was holding down a good job with a fine and well-respected company. They had a good life. Occasionally, they attended company functions in London. They both appreciated fine wine and gourmet food. Their circle of friends was varied and many of them had interests in the Arts.

Only last week, Arthur had told her that they had been invited to a dinner being held at a prestigious London restaurant for the company's most successful salesmen.

She was conscious of the fact that Arthur would need to look the part as he was one of the company's best salesmen. She would have his suit cleaned and would buy herself a new dress for the occasion.

Arthur took pride in his appearance and always insisted on a sharp crease in his trousers. The two suits which he used in business were always kept in tip top condition. When he stayed overnight on one of his 'business trips' he always returned home with the suit he had taken with him still looking as though it had not been worn.

She decided that the following morning she would take the chosen suit to the cleaners. That would just leave her to find a new dress to wear for this very special occasion.

It was Friday and the sun was out. It was going to be a nice day. She was in a good mood which probably meant that she would find a nice dress without too much trouble. Arthur had left at his usual time. She had the day off and was going to use it to treat herself.

Opening the large wardrobe which they shared, she took his suit out and laid it on the bed. To make sure Arthur hadn't left any coins in the pockets, she started slipping her hand into the trouser pockets. They were empty. She then checked the inside pocket of the jacket. There was something there. It felt like paper. Good job she had checked before taking it to the cleaners.

Drawing the item out, she saw it was an envelope. Perhaps it was the name and details of a new customer. She put it on the bedside table.

Folding the suit up to make it easier to take out, she looked at the bedside clock and was surprised it was already 10 o'clock. She had decided to have a slow and relaxing start to the day and had taken more time than usual over breakfast. She felt almost guilty about the time she had wasted and decided then to get herself ready to go out.

Things were going well.

After leaving Arthur's suit at the cleaners, she had found the perfect dress for the function they were going to attend.

By 2 o'clock she had made her way home. A quiet cup of tea and sandwich was all she wanted. She sat in the living room looking out of the window at the manicured lawn and the trees waving their branches in the slight breeze. How lucky she was.

In Francis Road, Beryl was sitting on her bed. She wasn't sure what she felt. The house was very quiet. She felt almost suffocated by the silence.

Her room was the same as when she had left. The things on her dressing table hadn't been moved. The bedspread was lying smoothed across the bed. The crucifix and chain were still on the little table by the bed. It was as if she had just stepped out for a while and was now back.

Her thoughts were trying to make sense of what had happened in the last couple of days. Why had she ended up back where she started? She could only remember snatches of the previous days. What had happened during that time?

Would she see Tom again? She could tell him how confused she felt. Her mum and nan wouldn't understand. She felt like a trapped bird that had escaped but had now been caught again.

She slumped on the bed.

The front door slammed shut and she could hear George racing up the stairs. He burst into the bedroom.

"I heard you were back. What's been going on? Nobody would tell me where you've been. Are you pregnant? They are saying in the bakery that you are."

He was quite out of breath, having run home and climbed the stairs at break-neck speed.

Beryl gasped. She couldn't believe what he'd just said. She glared at him.

"No. I'm not pregnant and you had better tell all those busy bodies that. How dare they say such a thing."

She turned her head away and didn't want to look at him. She felt a failure. It was all going to be so good but, here she was back where she had started with nothing to show for it but embarrassment. She took a deep breath and pouted.

"For your information, I had some photos taken in a proper studio. The photographer was very professional. He had all the lights and equipment that you get in film studios. If the photos are good, I could get offers of work."

Why was she saying all this? Was it to make something out of her confusion?

Poor George. He looked quite disappointed.

"Oh! I thought you were going to be the talk of the street so that I could tell me mates I was your brother."

With sudden found anger, Beryl stood up and shoved him over.

"Get out of my room and don't ever come in it again."

He was up and gone in a flash.

Her mum and nan would be in soon. She'd wait for them to return before she went downstairs.

It was now 5 o'clock and Elaine Davenport was busying herself in the kitchen. Arthur would be home in about an hour. She was pleased with the dress she had bought today and was looking forward to showing it to him.

As usual, she liked to look nice for him and so went upstairs to brush her hair and to look at herself in the full-length bedroom mirror to make sure she was happy with her appearance. She finally sprayed a little perfume onto her neck.

She turned and noticed the envelope she had left on the bedside table. She took it downstairs and decided to put it behind the clock on the shelf. She'd mention it to Arthur in case it was something important.

It was only after breakfast the next morning that she noticed it again. Arthur had left early as he told her he had extra customers to see. She was due at work today and felt quite rested and happy that she had used her day off wisely.

She put the envelope on the kitchen table.

She would have to get ready for work soon or she would be late.

In the household of 4 Francis Road, Flo had already gone shopping and Mavis was thinking of making her visit to Woolworths to speak to Mrs Davenport. She wasn't sure what she was going to say to her but felt she would be sympathetic about the situation. She'd wait a while, hoping to be able to speak to her around lunchtime. There were plenty of things she could do indoors until then.

Elaine Davenport finished her cup of tea, picked up her bag and went over to the door where her coat was hanging. One last glance around the room to check everything was in order and she would go. Her eyes came to rest on the envelope. Was it important? Should she have reminded Arthur about it?

Putting her bag down, she picked the envelope up and peered inside. There seemed to be photos in there. She pulled them out.

What she was looking at were images of a young girl almost naked, smiling into the camera. She appeared to be posing in a teasing way on a bed.

Another photo showed her standing and wearing a dress that seemed to be floating around her body, revealing her breasts and naked buttocks.

Elaine Davenport's hands were now shaking. She sat down with a thump as a feeling of disgust and anger flooded her mind. She knew there were girls who posed for photos like these, but she had never actually seen any of them. Where had they come from?

She thought the images couldn't get any worse.

Another three photos were in the envelope. She drew them out, almost not wanting to touch them.

The image of this young girl, now completely naked, showed the moments when she was being subjected to the intimate fondling that she and Arthur had never been able to achieve.

The kitchen was silent but she was sure she could hear her own heart beating.

She looked away from the photos for a few seconds and then realized the young woman posing for them was Beryl.

The same Beryl that had left her job at Woolworths to find a future as a model.

She felt seized with both disgust and anger. How had Arthur got hold of such images? She took a deep breath and exhaled loudly to try to release her tension.

There was no way she could go to work today. She must telephone the store and pretend to be ill.

She knew where Beryl lived. That was where she would go. Her mother needed to know what her daughter had got caught up in. She would take the photos with her. She would confront Arthur tonight.

It was almost 10 o'clock. Flo had come back from shopping, heaving the well-worn bag onto the kitchen table. Mavis was in the garden at the back of the house. She'd used her morning to do some washing and was hanging the items out to dry.

Flo called out to her.

"We'll have to change that greengrocers we use. Their stuff is getting worse. It's a waste of money."

Pulling the shopping from the bag she dropped a packet of sugar. It hit the floor with a dull thud spilling out its contents.

"Oh! bloody hell. That's all we want. I've carted that back home only to have that happen."

Mavis came in.

"Never mind, Mum. We can get some of it back. The floor was washed this morning while you were out. I've kept meself busy. I want to go to see that Mrs Davenport at lunchtime to ask her if Beryl could go back there."

With Flo putting the rest of the shopping away and Mavis

on her hands and knees clearing up the sugar, things didn't seem that bad after all.

The front door was partly open as usual. Nobody in this street shut their doors.

Elaine Davenport had taken the bus and was now walking down Francis Road making a mental note of all the house numbers. Routine Rosie was also in the street and she was observing the stranger ahead of her. She was a well-dressed woman and she wondered why someone like that would be here. She didn't recognize her at all. The woman slowed down as she approached No. 4. Finding the front door partly open, she called out.

"Is anybody in? I'm looking for Mavis Taylor."

By this time, Routine Rosie had caught up. At that moment, Flo appeared in the open doorway.

"Can I help you?"

She didn't recognize Elaine Davenport as she had never met the woman.

"I was hoping to have a word with Mrs Taylor about Beryl. I was her supervisor at Woolworths."

Flo smiled.

"That's a coincidence. She was going to see you herself today. It's funny how things work out. Would you believe it. She'll be pleased to see you."

Elaine Davenport felt sure she wouldn't, but said no more. She was aware that the reason for her visit would devastate her.

Opening the door fully, Flo stepped aside to let the visitor in. She didn't know whether to show her into the kitchen where Mavis was still on her hands and knees clearing up the spilt sugar, or to leave her in the passage and call Mavis out. Just then, Mavis came to the doorway.

Rubbing her hands down her apron, she wasn't sure how to respond to the unexpected appearance of Beryl's boss.

Elaine Davenport realized the difficult situation she was in was not going to get any better and so decided she would speak first.

"I do apologize for visiting you without an invitation but there is something I need to speak to you about rather urgently."

Mavis stepped aside and gestured for her to go into the kitchen. Flo was almost trying not to be there and suggested she put the kettle on to make some tea. She'd have to get the best cups and saucers out of the cupboard for this.

Mavis sat on one side of the table and Elaine Davenport pulled a chair out and sat on the other side.

She put her handbag on the table.

Mavis blurted out, "Beryl's upstairs in her room. I can ask her to come down as you are here."

Elaine Davenport suddenly sat upright. She now seemed to look like someone's boss.

She drew the envelope slowly out of her handbag. Flo was in the scullery making the tea.

"Before I tell you why I'm here, I have to ask if you know any of Beryl's friends who would take advantage of her?"

Mavis frowned. She didn't understand the question.

"What do you mean?"

Elaine Davenport sat forward, leaning on the table.

"I have evidence that she is being used by some very nasty people."

Flo appeared with the teapot and cups and saucers all neatly positioned on a tray. She wanted to show Beryl's boss that they knew how to treat visitors. She intended placing the tray in the middle of the table but stood holding it so that a space could be made for it.

Elaine Davenport slowly pulled the photos out of the envelope and spaced them out in front of Mavis. Mavis looked at them and then shut her eyes and then opened them again, almost hoping that what she had seen wouldn't be there this time. She gasped and put both her hands up to her face shouting, "No!"

Flo peered at the photos and then seemed to lose all the grip she had on the tray as it crashed down onto the floor, scattering the now broken cups and saucers, the teapot finally reaching a chair leg losing not only its spout and handle but all its contents among the wreckage. The sound of the falling china echoing through the silence of the house brought Beryl rushing down the stairs.

Bursting into the kitchen, she was shocked at what she saw spread out on the table. The situation was frightening witnessing what had happened.

Mavis stood up. She pulled and dragged Beryl over to the table and forced her to look at the photos.

Shouting at her, she said, "What have you done to us? You have become a slut."

There was so much more she wanted to say but the words were trapped by anger and disgust. She simply couldn't form them.

Elaine Davenport gathered up the photos and placed them back in the envelope.

She stood up.

"I'm sorry I have had to do this, but I felt you should know that Beryl had got into some very bad company. I can't tell you how I got hold of the photos, but I can assure you they will go no further. I have my own demons to deal with."

She left a shocked household and hoped that Beryl's family would give her guidance.

Mavis was distressed. Beryl was confused, and Flo was hoping none of the neighbours ever got wind of what had happened. She wouldn't be able to face any of them again. Beryl was still standing by the table, innocence etched on her face. She was just beginning to realize that her dreams of becoming a model might be over.

Later that evening Flo and Mavis were still feeling totally wound up and wondering if they could have prevented all this. Why had Beryl allowed herself to be used like that? Elaine Davenport had not seemed as shocked as they had been. Thank goodness they could trust her about all this.

Elaine Davenport, on the other hand, was wondering if those photos would come back to haunt Beryl in the future. She hoped not.

CHAPTER SEVEN

The following morning Annie was wondering why Flo hadn't appeared in her doorway. She knew the wedding arrangements meeting had taken place the night before. It was very unlike her to miss out on up-to-date news. Annie was glad she had such a good friend to confide in. Flo never seemed phased by anything. Perhaps it was because she was a widow and had taken on the decisions her own daughter needed to confront and make. She had been the mainstay of the household for years. She always seemed to see problems in black and white. Face them and a solution would be forthcoming. She needed to see her today to tell her what had been said at the meeting. She needed some advice.

Fred had left for work having had a sleepless night. He hadn't said much but she knew he was worried about the expense of the wedding.

John had gone back to the flat having had a rude awakening to the problems he was going to have to deal with. He was hoping the foreman at the site would be able to fix him up with work that didn't involve too much lifting and shifting. His hand would be out of action for about a month. If he didn't work, he wouldn't get paid.

Christine's parents seemed to be on a roller coaster trip that was speeding faster by the minute. He knew they wanted the wedding to take place as soon as possible but if he was to find a couple of rooms where him and Christine could live, he would need time to sort that out.

Annie glanced at the clock. It was half past 12. Fred wouldn't be back until about 5.

Perhaps Flo was ill. No. Mavis would have told her. Perhaps she ought to go to her. She could do some shopping on her way.

She ran a comb through her hair and put her comfy shoes on. She looked out of the scullery window and it looked quite bright. She wouldn't need a coat, only her cardigan.

Pulling the door shut, she didn't bother to lock it.

Without turning around, she could hear the familiar clank of one of the wheels on Bridget's bike. She'd only gone a few paces when the sound came to a halt next to her. She liked Bridget. She'd been a midwife in this area for years. Before the NHS was formed, anyone having a baby had to rely on women who knew a bit about childbirth and they didn't always get things right. Sometimes mothers were lost in the process. She had tried to teach some of the nurses who were training during the war years but not all of them were used for births. The hospitals were mostly flooded with badly injured men on their return home. Things had improved now in 1953. Nurses had received training in maternity and childcare procedures.

Once the war had ended, husbands were returning and the birthrate had spiraled. She had even contemplated retiring from it all as sometimes she was out all day and all night bringing this new generation into the world. However, here she was, still working.

"Hello Annie. I heard you had a bit of a fire the other evening. Good job it was spotted before there was any damage."

She smiled and her face lit up.

"You had the luck of the Irish there when you think about it. All those bombs during the war without even a cracked window. It would have been sod's law if the fire had taken hold and burnt you down."

"Bridget, don't say such a thing. It was only some stuff caught in the chimney that created the fire. It wasn't much at all."

She didn't want this conversation to continue because Bridget was bound to ask why they had lit a fire in the front room anyway. She wasn't sure how much of a rumour was going around about John's pregnant girlfriend. Surely, if Bridget had heard anything, she would have mentioned it.

Starting to walk on, Annie had to get away.

"I've got to go. I need to get to the shops and then call in on Flo and Mavis."

Bridget took the hint and they went their separate ways.

Shopping was the last thing on her mind. She quickened her pace and reached No. 4. She pushed on the front door as usual. It didn't budge. She pushed it again. That was strange. They only shut it when they went to bed. She tried to look through the net curtain covering the front window but she couldn't see anything. She bent down and tried to peer through the iron letterbox but that didn't make matters any clearer. They must both be out. Perhaps they were visiting Beryl wherever she now lived.

She felt quite conspicuous just standing there. She didn't know what to do.

Just then she saw Routine Rosie plodding along the street.

Annie turned. “I’m glad I’ve seen you. I was hoping to have a word with Flo but she seems to be out. Have you seen her?”

Rosie was only too pleased to have found someone to talk to. She mumbled something but Annie couldn’t hear what it was.

“What did you say?”

Rosie stepped closer.

“There’s something going on. I saw a very smart woman go in there yesterday. I didn’t recognize her.”

Then, pointing to the front step, she said, “Flo hasn’t done the step and window ledge today. She never misses that.”

She then patted the side of her nose.

“If your routine is upset, that means you don’t get the time back. A bad thing that is. I should know. My life has been interrupted a few times and I dwell on that. There’s not much you can tell me about routines.”

Annie had heard enough.

“I’ll call on her later.”

Before Rosie could say any more, Annie carried on down the street to the shops. There couldn’t be much wrong or she would have heard.

Beryl was back in her room feeling confused and hurt. She was only now learning how Ann had helped to get her to hospital. Flo had told her what had been happening during her time with Tom. Her mum and nan had got it all wrong. She was feeling more annoyed by the minute. They had messed everything up. She didn’t need to be rescued. They had ruined her chance to be a model.

Stomping back down the stairs, she burst into the kitchen

and took them by surprise. She took a deep breath. Staring at the two of them, she screamed, "You don't know what you've done. I had a chance to be a model and you've just ruined it. Those photos were what models pose for. Tom was very pleased with them. I could have got job offers when the right people got to see them."

She was shouting and running out of breath.

"I didn't need rescuing. I didn't need Ann to be involved. She promised she wouldn't say anything to anyone about it. What sort of a friend has she turned out to be?"

She raised her hand and, pointing a finger at the two of them, she shouted, "You won't stop me. I'll go again. This time you won't find me. I'll make sure of that."

Flo and Mavis hadn't uttered a word. They just sat there listening to this tirade.

Beryl, now fuming, turned and ran up the stairs. The sound of her bedroom door slamming made them jump and the cups on the table rattle.

In the sudden silence of the kitchen, all Flo could think of was Nel next door must have heard every word that Beryl had spat out. How would they both be able to face the neighbours again? She thought she had the situation under control but it was all going wrong.

Going over to the dresser, she opened the top drawer and got the front door key out. Without saying a word, she went along the small passage and locked the door. That would mean they only had to watch the scullery door which led into the garden to stop any escape. There must be a key for that somewhere in the dresser. She would try to find it. They wouldn't be going out today.

Fred had left for work this morning with the intention of asking around about weddings and costs. There was always someone among the dockers he worked with who had found themselves with the same problem he and Annie now faced. He didn't want to borrow the money. He'd heard some nightmare stories about that when the money couldn't be repaid on time. He remembered Jim Venables saying they thought their guests, including themselves, would be 16. Fred and Annie had counted the people they thought should be there and it was 10 including the two of them. Jim Venables had mentioned that he had some arrangement with the steward at The British Legion Hall who would be able to do him a good deal. They wouldn't provide the drinks though and so they would have to come from somewhere else. If Vera was going to arrange for the bans to be read and deal with the bride's dress and the bridesmaids' dresses, Annie would be able to get Anthea, the W.I. woman, to do the flowers. That only left the cake to be dealt with. It all seemed to be never ending.

Once he'd had a word with a couple of the blokes on his shift who he knew had been put through the same wringer that he was caught up in, he'd have a better idea of how much money he was going to have to find. There would have to be another meeting with the Venables.

Making her way back from the shops, Annie decided to have another go at seeing Flo. This time she called through the letterbox because the door was still firmly shut.

Suddenly the sound of the key turning in the lock was a relief. The door opened, and Flo stood there looking almost rigid.

Annie blurted out "What's going on? Has something

happened?"

Without saying a word, Flo almost pulled her into the passage.

"Go into the kitchen and keep your voice down. Walls have ears."

During the next half hour, Annie was brought up to date with things. Once both Flo and Mavis had finished airing, what they thought was pure filth, they both felt released from the nightmare they considered they had experienced.

"You should have seen those photos. They were like the ones dirty old men pay money for. That supervisor woman told us they wouldn't go any further, thank God. We didn't ask her how she came by them."

Having taken it all in, Annie said, "Where's Beryl now then?"

Mavis pointed up to the ceiling. "She's in her room. We've locked the front door, as you know, so she can't get out. Poor George has to knock when he comes home from work."

Annie was now feeling as though her problems were nothing compared to what they'd told her.

She explained how the meeting had gone and that everything seemed to be heading for a wedding in about six weeks. The bride should only be starting to show by then.

"Fred is trying to find out what our share is going to cost. He's not looking well with the worry of it all. John is trying to find a couple of rooms for him and this girl to live in."

She already didn't like her.

"Do you know, she even said she wants to go away after the wedding. You know. Have a night somewhere."

Mavis gave a knowing look.

"She's lucky she's not sick with the pregnancy. Most people are at her stage. I take it she has been told by a doctor that she's pregnant."

Annie suddenly felt a wave of fright come over her.

Frowning, she said, "You don't think she's pretending to be pregnant just to get John to marry her. How would we know if she's just trapping him?"

The silence in the room said it all. Nobody knew what to say.

Suddenly they could hear movement upstairs. What was Beryl doing?

Annie decided she didn't want to see Beryl. She wouldn't know what to say to her.

"I'd better get going. I seem to have been out for a long time."

She left Flo and Mavis still sitting at the table as though they were dreading what was going to happen next.

Walking back home, her thoughts were now focusing on what Mavis had said. She wanted Fred to be back from work so that she could tell him about it. She was getting more worked up just thinking about it all.

Her silent thoughts were racing. She'd never even thought the girl could be tricking John. Even her parents had accepted that she was pregnant. What had she told them?

Reaching her front door, she felt almost relieved. She needed the familiarity of home.

Silently putting her shopping away in the cupboards, she stood for a moment, clutching the ketchup bottle. That was an essential in this family because her other two boys, Roger and Ken, would plaster loads of the stuff over every meal she cooked for them. How lucky she was that, although they were now teenagers, they both seemed to stay out of trouble. In fact, when they had been told about the wedding, they never asked any questions. It was as though they already knew about the pregnancy.

The shopping now stored, her thoughts transferred to Sarah. She still hadn't been told about things. If the truth were told, Annie felt embarrassed about letting her know because the whole situation seemed cheap and nasty. She didn't want Sarah's adoptive family to think badly of them.

She went into the front room. Looking out of the window she could see One-leg Len making his way home having been out to place his bets at the bookies in the high road. Today he was using a crutch to help him on his way, the hospital having suggested he use it because the new NHS were getting more and more things now to help people like him.

Looking around the room, she decided that the next meeting with Jim and Vera Venables would he held without the fire being lit. It almost seemed like an omen that with the latest thoughts going around in her head.

Back in the kitchen she was wishing the time away because she wanted to know what Fred had been able to find out and she also had the troubling question to speak to him about whether the girl was really pregnant.

At the home of Elaine and Arthur Davenport, an inquisition was being carried out. Although Elaine was shocked by the photos she had found, she was a woman with a past that her husband wasn't aware of. She, too, had been tricked into allowing a boyfriend to take photos of her semi-naked on the understanding that the two of them would become engaged to be married. She had trusted him. He had betrayed that trust and had shown the photos to all his friends. Although this was twenty years earlier, she still could not forget the horror she felt and had decided then to take charge of her own life and never be used by a man again. That was why she couldn't indulge in the sort of intimacies and fondling that had been displayed in Beryl's photos. Arthur had come to accept during their marriage that such acts of love could never be achieved between them. His wife always held back but, of course, he never knew why.

So far as the photos were concerned, he was a good story teller and explained that he had unwittingly taken possession of them for a friend whose marriage was in trouble and the friend wanted them out of the house in case his wife found them.

Why, he asked Elaine, would he have left them at their home where she would find them?

He felt quite pleased with himself, having explained away their existence. He said he would return them to his friend!

Beryl stood looking out of her bedroom window. The small garden at the back of the house was looking more boring than usual to her. The seemingly endless strips of land were only punctuated by the occasional home-made shed or chicken run. She felt like a prisoner with no prospect of escape. She was annoyed with herself for ending up where she had started. She would have to do something.

George had told her that the front door was now locked, and he thought the scullery door had been locked as well. Flo always took the keys up to bed with her lately. He still hadn't been told what all the fuss was about and was annoyed that he now had to knock on the front door to get in.

If she was to escape it would have to be when they were all in bed and it would have to be through the scullery window over the sink. Could she fit through it?

Mavis was now calling up the stairs that if she wanted something to eat, she'd have to come down now or go hungry.

If she went down, she'd be able to have a better look at the scullery window. Hopefully, she'd be able to get through it.

She was feeling a bit better now that she'd made up her mind that she would go ahead with this plan. She'd pack a small bag with essentials.

The meal was eaten almost in silence. Mavis and Flo were chatting about Fred and Annie. Apparently, they had some sort of problem at their house.

George couldn't wait to go out to see his mates and get away from all this. He'd ask Beryl what was going on when he saw her tomorrow.

Back in her bedroom, Beryl was ready to go.

She waited patiently, listening to all the familiar sounds in the house which were what she would have to avoid if she managed to get out. The floorboard outside her gran and mum's room always creaked when you walked over it. She'd also have to tread as far over to the left on the third stair from the top because it always made a thumping sound. So far as she could remember, the bannister running the length of the stairs shouldn't be touched or it would make a soft creaking alarm. If she got as far as the kitchen undetected there were no sound traps she would have to avoid.

She looked at the clock by the bed. It was half past twelve.

She knew George was in and tucked up for the night. She could hear her gran snoring and knew her mum always slept with the quilt pulled up around her face to block out the sound. If she didn't go now, it would be too late. She was still wondering if she could get away with it. Cautiously, she began her journey.

She left her room without even a backward glance.

It took no time to reach the kitchen. She crept towards the scullery, hardly daring to breathe. The sink was empty except for the washing up bowl and the draining board was clear. She'd have to somehow get onto that to be able to slip the latch on the window. She'd have to stand on a chair. Once the window was open, she could drop her bag out onto the path below. Her mum and gran had the room at the front of the house and so they wouldn't hear it hit the ground.

She would then have to try to sit on the window ledge with her legs outside so that she could lower herself down.

She'd forgotten that there were always things on the window ledge including the washing up bottle, the tin with the tapers which they lit to use on the gas stove when the kettle or saucepans were on it. Her mum also had an old ash tray there as well in which she collected drawing pins and elastic bands and any odd bits of string. It seemed a thing she did during the war years and continued doing it.

Moving all these obstacles, she mounted the chair and put the plan into action.

The bag went first and she surprised herself that it was very easy to get through the window.

Where their garden came to an end, the back gardens of the houses behind theirs were only separated by a small alley.

In the moonlight that night a figure could be seen standing

by a shed, a cigarette end glowing as he drew on it. Not a sound could be heard and this shadow didn't move. He observed the figure of, what seemed to be a girl, climbing out of the window. He drew on the cigarette again.

The moon was gradually being covered by thin cloud, making it difficult for him to follow the girl's progress. He waited for it to pass.

Standing silently like a sentry, he peered over to the garden again, a watery moonlight now rippling in the sky but there was nobody there. He smiled.

Perhaps this was a frantic but, well planned effort to escape an awful situation. Maybe the girl was eloping. People still did that. Did she have a plan? Had she been working on it for some time?

She had certainly chosen a good night for it. There was just enough light to be able to see a path. He wondered where she was heading. The other occupants of that house would be baffled by her absence no doubt.

She had taken the time to quietly close the window before picking up the bag and disappearing into the night. The only thing she couldn't do anything about would be the telltale evidence of the misplaced chair and the shifted items from the window ledge.

Outside in the damp of the night, the shadowed figure felt almost excited that he had witnessed a great escape. It felt personal to him. He secretly hoped the girl had enough money to get her away. He hoped she had planned this well. He hoped her plan would work. It deserved to be a success. His mundane life had suddenly been interrupted by this short-lived incident.

He turned and entered his own scullery. This anonymous

person had awakened distant memories of his own youth. He would finally go to bed with an unexpected smile on his face.

The morning was greeted with a stunned silence. Flo stood by the sink and stared at the situation in front of her. The chair said it all. She guessed what had occurred while the rest of the household were asleep.

She immediately made a beeline for George. He swore he knew nothing about Beryl's plans.

For some reason, Mavis felt she needed to stand at the front door looking up and down the street. She instinctively knew she had lost Beryl for now.

When you take a window seat in most small cafes, you can quietly witness passers-by all seeming to have a path to follow. The truth is, there are no paths. Paths are made by walking.

The cup of tea in front of her had stopped giving off its heat. It had now taken on the look of a tepid pool. Looking across the room, the unobstructed haze of cigarette smoke swirled and then disappeared, leaving only its odour.

She had been sitting here for only half an hour, and yet, she was beginning to feel that she knew the people who were her unexpected companions. They chatted to their friends and she unwittingly overheard about their trials and tribulations being shared. Some of their news was good and brought laughter and some was of troubles which needed an answer. How good it must be to have friends to confide in.

The clatter of the cups and saucers made the place seem like home and yet she was on her own among strangers.

Grace felt she had reached some sort of crossroads in her life. She wanted out.

The café she had chosen this morning had not been a

planned one. It was simply in a street she was walking along.

Tom and Martine would be wondering where she was. That would not be because they were worried about her but because there would be things to be done.

She now felt she wanted her freedom. Her time spent in the library had left her with a feeling of being trapped in isolation. She must make a break away from Tom, Martine and that studio. It wouldn't be easy. They wouldn't understand.

The few possessions she had at the flat could easily fit into one case. She would plan her escape and choose the moment to collect her things, leaving a note for the others.

Her next thought was where she would go.

She didn't want a large town or city because that would only be swapping one place for the same thing. She would choose somewhere on the coast that might need staff. She didn't care what the job was. Hotels would be worth trying. The money she had been saving would be enough for a train ticket to freedom. She was now beginning to wish she had someone to talk things over with just like her unexpected café companions had.

Still staring out of the window, she was startled by the voice of an elderly gentleman which seemed directed at her.

"Would you mind if I shared your table? There don't appear to be any other free seats."

He smiled.

"Oh, please do. I'll be leaving in a minute anyway."

He sat down opposite her. The newspaper he was holding had been neatly folded as though he had already finished with it. She didn't want to look at him in case he started up a conversation. She didn't know him and didn't particularly want to.

He ordered a tea and a slice of cake.

Grace sat silently trying to compose in her mind the letter she would leave for Tom and Martine. She was staring into space with her eyes screwed up as though that would help. What could she say?

She must have been frowning because the elderly gentleman asked if she was all right. This was a stranger showing concern for her.

"Yes, I'm fine thank you. I was just trying to think what I could say in a goodbye letter to some friends."

The waitress arrived with his tea and cake. He stirred the tea slowly as though he too was thinking about something.

Looking up he said "If they are your friends, you don't need to say goodbye, just that you are going to be away for a while. You must never say goodbye to friends."

She sat back on her seat. She knew what she was going to do.

CHAPTER EIGHT

At No. 48 Annie almost pounced on Fred as he came through the kitchen doorway. He'd had a bad day at the docks. There had been a fight between two blokes who started by swearing and shouting at each other but then it had descended into punches being thrown. Fred had stood back, together with a lot of the others, watching it all, but it wasn't long before the dock's gangmaster intervened to put a stop to it. Just watching what grown men were capable of once they began an argument always scared him. Johnny was becoming just like them. He's going to have to control his temper once he's married.

Annie didn't waste any time.

"Do you know what Mavis said when I told her about that girl wanting to go away for a night once the wedding was over? She started me thinking, I can tell you. Never mind the expense. Where does she think Johnny's going to get the money for that? He's still looking for somewhere they can live. That won't come cheap."

She was now getting out of breath. That happened every time she got worked up.

Fred was still standing in the kitchen doorway. He hadn't spoken a word. His face said it all.

Annie finally came to a gasping halt. The kitchen seemed to have run out of air for her to suck in.

"What the bloody hell are you going on about? I've had a

gut full of other people today and I don't want it in me own kitchen."

He walked passed Annie and headed to the scullery to wash his hands as if he was trying to wash the day away. As he walked, he ran his fingers through his hair. That wasn't a good sign. Annie remained silent. She hadn't even put the kettle on for his tea yet.

Only seconds passed but it seemed like minutes. Finally, Fred emerged from the scullery.

"What the hell are you going on about? What has Mavis been saying? Her and Flo ought to mind their own business. I don't know why you listen to them."

Annie decided to answer him back which she didn't usually do but things seemed to be getting out of control. There was so much to think about and sort out. She thought her brain would burst.

"How do we know if that girl really is pregnant? We've taken her word for it. We don't know her. Has she shown any signs of being pregnant? Has she suffered the usual sickness at the start of it? You know what I was like with ours. She reckons she is two months gone. It's only then that you usually go to the doctors. What happens if they get married and then she finds out it's been a false alarm? These things happen you know. Johnny will be well and truly trapped. I've heard about girls like her. How many boyfriends has she had?"

She was getting out of breath again. She slumped into the chair by the fire. She didn't know whether to laugh or cry.

Fred drew in a deep breath. He was the one feeling like he was in a trap. What with Annie, Johnny, the Venables and that nosey Mavis. Annie was making herself ill with it all and it hadn't kicked off yet.

In roles reversed, Fred decided to make Annie a cup of tea. She really needed a proper drink but that was out of the question. The only drink they kept in the house was sherry and that had been drunk by Vera Venables when they were here for the meeting. The thoughts running through his mind weren't good. Bloody Vera Venables had lorded it when she was here. She had tried to make out that Christine had been taken by Johnny against her will. That was bloody rubbish because she was even egging him on when they were all trying to sort things out. How many times had she been around the block he wondered?

Passing the cup of tea to Annie who was still caught up in her own turmoil of thoughts, he decided that he would have to have a meeting with Johnny and Jim Venables to make sure everything was kosher. He wouldn't include the women. There could be a lot of straight talking. He wanted to get things sorted before they went any further.

"Once I've had something to eat, love, I'll get meself round to The Wagon and Horses because I know that's where Johnny drinks. I'll see if he's in there. I want a word with him."

Annie immediately knew Fred was feeling things were out of control. He never went out in the evening.

It was getting dark when Fred reached The Wagon and Horses. The smell of the place wafted over him long before he reached it. The doors were fully open as usual and the noise coming from the place would be enough to guide a blind man to it. The pub had been on this corner since his own father was around. The lights which shone through the grimy glass of the windows were the same ones that even Hitler couldn't extinguish. The place had defiantly escaped some of the worst bombings in the area. Its cellars had housed and protected the street's occupants during the air raids.

He didn't feel at ease now in these places. When he was a lot younger, they were more like meeting places after work when you could have a drink and get any grievances out in the open before going home. Looking around, most of the people in here were of a different generation. Fathers had been replaced by sons.

He went over to the crowded bar and ordered a pint of Best Bitter. Looking around, he couldn't see anywhere he could sit in seclusion and so decided he'd stay put and wait, hopefully, for Johnny to make an appearance. He felt sure he'd be in at any time.

He was vacantly staring into his beer when someone called his name.

"Fred. We don't usually see you in here, especially this time of the day."

He turned. It was Alan, an old school friend. He recognized him immediately. Many a scrap he'd had with him in the playground. He'd filled out a lot and Fred guessed he was fond of a pint or two by the stomach hanging over the belt of his trousers.

Coming over to Fred, he said, "How's things with you? Are you still at the docks? I don't get about much around here since we moved from the flat. We're in one of those new prefabs they put up. Bloody marvellous they are."

Fred didn't know whether to be pleased he'd met an old mate or not. He wasn't really in a mood to be social. He'd have to seem pleased to see him. He'd let Alan do the talking.

"Well. How about seeing you again after such a time. When did we last meet up? It must be at least five years."

Fred sipped his beer. He wasn't in a mood to gulp it down in case he was offered another.

"How's the family and your Annie? She had her hands full with your lads last time I heard. They're all at work now I suppose."

Fred drew in a deep breath.

"Yeah, they're doing all right. What about your girls? They must have left school by now. Are they still living at home?"

That put a broad smile on Alan's face.

"We've been lucky with them. They both got places at Grammar School and they're deciding what to do about jobs. One of them wants to be a doctor and the other one wants to be an accountant. Can you imagine that?"

Fred finally finished his beer.

"I'm hoping to see our Johnny while I'm here. He usually comes in about now."

Above the conversational din of the place, Fred heard Alan's name being called.

"I think someone's trying to get your attention."

Alan turned and waved over to someone.

"I'd better go. It was good to see you again. I saw your Johnny in The Star about half an hour ago. He was talking to that Irish girl, Niamh. I don't know for sure, but she looked in the family way. I didn't even know she'd got married. Nice girl that."

He left Fred standing at the bar. He had to get out of this place. He felt so fired up with anger. Why was Johnny talking to the Irish girl? He had no reason to be meeting up with her or buying her a drink.

Almost stumbling out of the pub's doorway, he decided he'd head for The Star. It was only a few streets away.

It was getting dark now, just like his mood. His pace quickened. He wanted to get there before Johnny left.

The questions kept flying around in his mind. It would take some good answers to satisfy Fred's suspicions. He prided himself on being fair whatever the situation but now he was doubting everything. He turned the corner and had reached The Star.

It was only a small pub. Before going in he looked through the window. It was far more orderly than The Wagon and Horses. This was a place you could take your wife or girlfriend. The bar had some order about it with the brass pumps shining like beacons, the bar polished and protected by bar mats laid neatly along its length. The metal shelf above it was orderly, packed with glinting glasses waiting and ready for the next customer. Sure enough, standing at the bar was Johnny, deep in conversation with Niamh. Fred still hung back, wanting to observe them both. He felt guilty.

He remembered Niamh when she first came to the area. She was beautiful. For a while she had sung in one of the local dance halls on a Saturday night. Her voice was as clear as a bell. She had a way about her that made her very popular with the local lads.

Her auburn hair would swing across her shoulders and her smiling eyes seemed to have no background and haunted you. Her Catholic upbringing was down to the nuns but that hadn't dampened her spirit. Her local priest had scolded her for not coming to church more often to see him. Her thoughts were, it's the confession not the priest that gives absolution. In any case, she didn't have anything to confess.

Niamh was looking at Johnny and smiling. He bought her another drink. They seemed to be happy and relaxed in each other's company.

Fred looked away as a couple brushed passed him and went in. He must decide what to do. He couldn't hang around outside the pub or it would seem strange.

He looked in again just as Johnny was passing an envelope to Niamh. She accepted it and smiled at him. She didn't look inside the envelope as though she knew what it contained. She then kissed him, finished her drink and, picking her bag up, headed for the door.

Fred didn't know what to do. Should he walk away? Should he turn his back so that his face couldn't be seen?

He was sure Niamh would recognize him if he didn't.

He decided to walk a few paces along the street hoping she would go in the other direction. She did. He'd never felt so relieved. Once she was out of sight, he went into the place and up to the bar. It was now or never.

Johnny turned his back to the door and leaned over the bar. Fred walked over to him but stayed silent. Johnny turned.

"What are you doing here? Is everything all right? Is something wrong with Mum?"

Fred recognized Johnny's expression when he was confronted with a situation. It hadn't changed since he was a youngster.

"I want a word with you while we're on our own. Get me a beer. We need to talk.

The abrupt message was recognized as something to worry about.

Going over to a small table under the window, Fred sat down. He was in no mood to mince his words.

Bringing the drinks over, Johnny cautiously sat down.

"What's up then?"

Fred started. "Me and your mother want to know if that girl, Christine, is actually pregnant. Is she just trying to haul you in and you've been caught? How do you know for sure, if she is pregnant, that it's yours? Have you worked out when it could have happened? Were you seeing her a couple of months ago?"

The questions continued to be fired at an astonished and silent Johnny.

"Could she have been seeing someone else at the same time as you? She's not just trying to get away from her domineering father, is she?"

Johnny stayed silent, not knowing what to answer first.

Fred took a sip of his beer. Placing the glass down firmly on the table, the beer spilled over the top of the glass. As the small pool reached an ashtray, he stretched his hand across the table and flicked the beer onto the floor. His every movement signalled to Johnny that this was going to be a tense meeting.

Before Johnny could utter a word, Fred continued.

"I just saw you with that Irish girl, Niamh. Where does she fit into this story? You gave her an envelope which she seemed to be expecting."

He picked up his beer again, pausing before he put it to his lips. He put it down again.

Staring at Johnny, only inches from his face, he carried on

with the questions and doubts.

"You won't be the first bloke to be trapped into marriage, you know. You've just got to be sure you've got your facts right."

He paused, hoping Johnny would say something to prove his concerns were right.

Johnny was sitting with his back against the wall. It was almost a sign.

As if on cue, Johnny suddenly found his voice.

"You know that nurse woman, the Irish one, well she stopped me to ask how Mum was as she seemed to think she wasn't well. I told her she was all right and that I was going to be a father soon which Mum was chuffed about. After I told her about Christine, she seemed a bit confused because she knew nothing about Christine being pregnant. She definitely hadn't been in to see the doc because, if she had, she would know about it."

Gulping his beer down, Johnny was just beginning to think that, maybe, he had been caught up in a situation where Christine was determined to get married, no matter what. Her best friend had just got engaged and she felt she was being left behind. She'd been seeing Italian Tony on and off for a few weeks as well as him, but Tony had sussed out what Christine's game was and didn't want any more to do with her.

Johnny suddenly seemed to come alive. "You know, Dad, when I think about it, she can't be pregnant by me anyway, because the only time we had it off was on the night her best friend got engaged and that was six weeks ago."

Fred was getting more and more worried about what he was going to hear. He was getting embarrassed.

Johnny continued.

"If she says she's two months gone, it's probably Italian Tony's kid."

Although this was what Fred wanted to hear, he was wondering how he was going to tell Jim Venables that he was barking up the wrong tree. He would, with this information from Johnny, be calling his daughter a liar about the situation. Jim Venables wouldn't take to that very well.

Fred looked around the place. He was trying to find a distraction from all this information. The trouble was, the people who used this place were quiet and seemed to be using it as a club for quiet moments.

"Right. That's what I want to hear. Jim Venables will have to be told."

The atmosphere between them had suddenly been lifted.

"I'll get word to him somehow that there's some sorting out to be done. I don't want the women there and I won't give him more than he needs to know, but I want this bloody mess sorted. There's no way we're going to fork out for a wedding when it looks as though that wop couldn't keep it in his trousers."

Johnny was shocked at the brutal way his dad was talking.

"Don't say anything to your mother or Harry. It looks as though you've been stitched up and it could get nasty. I'll arrange a meet. I'd better get back or your mother will be wondering what's going on. Remember, stay stumm (or schtum)."

Niamh was making her way home to her grandmother's house. The envelope Johnny had given her was safe in her bag. She wasn't sure what she was feeling, only that she was grateful her grandmother had insisted she stay with her until she had to go to the convent hospital to have the baby. Beyond that, she wasn't sure how her life would evolve. The money would pay for some baby things and would be enough to pay her grandmother for her help. Her own parents had both been killed during the war. It was only by chance she had learnt that, because they had both been blown to smithereens during a bombing. Two lives lost in the old world in anger and now one trying to survive in a new world of love. There was no doubt Johnny had fathered this child. If she had insisted he marry her, she would forever wonder if he truly loved her, but then, she knew that.

Things seemed to have become complicated when Father Ignatius learned from the Sisters that Niamh had become, what he called, 'a fallen woman'. It had been his idea that she give birth to the child at the convent hospital and that, when the child was six weeks old, it would be offered for adoption. This is what she didn't want. She needed the Sisters to help her give birth, although she wasn't entirely sure that was necessary because if she remained at her grandmother's house, surely Bridgit would come to her assistance.

Annie was sitting by the fire which was struggling to keep it's dying embers glowing. She hadn't bothered to put the light on. The red glow from the fire had given the room a look of sunset. She closed her eyes and her mind turned to thoughts of the Venables family and what it might be like to have to include them into their family meetings. This was not how she imagined the news of a first grandchild would be.

Where was Fred? He'd been gone for ages.

Just then, she heard the familiar sound of the key in the

lock.

Fred stood in front of her.

"Well. I think we can rest assured that the baby is not Johnny's."

Annie pulled herself up in the chair.

"What! How do you know that?"

"I've just spent some time with Johnny and between us we've worked out the timing's not right. He thinks it must be Italian Tony's. You know what that means? We've got to arrange a meeting with Jim Venables to stop these wedding arrangements. That's going to be murder. I'll get word to him tomorrow. I don't want him around here."

He dropped down onto the kitchen chair. Annie didn't know what to say. She had plenty of questions to ask but she could see Fred was so tired. At least he'd made his mind up that he could get it all sorted out.

As tired as he was, lying in bed Fred couldn't free his mind of how to approach Jim Venables. Among the turmoil of his thoughts he realized that Johnny hadn't told him where Niamh fitted in. Why did he meet up with her? Why did he give her an envelope? What was in it? What was that for?

On the building site the next morning, Johnny had arrived. He hoped the foreman could give him work that wouldn't aggravate his hand injury. It had been playing him up.

He heard his name being called out and turned to see one of the bricklayers beckoning him over.

"Wotcha, Johnny. If you're still looking for a couple of rooms, I know where you can get them. A mate of mine needs to rent a couple out in his gaff because he needs the money."

"Hello, mate. Thanks all the same, but I won't be needing

them now. My luck seems to have changed."

The brickie looked confused.

"What's happened then? She hasn't gone and lost the kid, has she? Does this mean you're not getting cut and carried?"

Johnny was beaming.

"You're right there. It turns out the kid can't be mine. She was seeing Italian Tony before me. Her old man isn't going to be too chuffed. At least I'm off the hook."

As Fred went through the dock gates, he was wondering how he was going to get in touch with Jim Venables. He had to see him tonight. It couldn't wait.

As luck would have it, one of the stevedores had heard that Jim's daughter was going to marry Fred's son and he came over to congratulate him on the prospect of becoming a grandfather.

Without giving anything away, Fred asked if he knew how to get in touch with Jim during the day.

"You can get a message to him at the British Legion Club. The steward there's got a phone number for him."

As soon as Fred's shift was over, he made his way to the British Legion Club. It turned out that it was in an old church building not too far away.

He had always felt it was something a bit classy in these places because of the way they were spoken of. They apparently held a lot of what people called 'functions'. Jim Venables had mentioned the place several times when they had last met.

Once inside, it reminded Fred of the Town Hall. There were wood panelled walls, loads of framed certificates and what looked like an engraved Roll of Honour. Walking through the entrance hall, he could see a well-stocked bar and, luckily, there was someone behind it.

The barman looked up as Fred approached.

"I'm hoping to contact Jim Venables urgently and I was told you've got a phone number for him."

The barman put the cloth down that he was polishing the glasses with.

"Yeah. That's right. He comes in here a couple of times a week. In fact, he's due in tonight because we're doing his daughter's reception for him. She's getting married in a few weeks. If you come in about 8, you'll find him at the bar. Shall I say you're looking for him? What's the name?"

He picked the cloth up and continued polishing the glasses.

"No. That's all right mate. I'll be in later. Thanks."

As he made his way out, he noticed how smart the place was. The polished chairs around the small tables were all set in an orderly way. A huge cabinet along one wall had a collection of photos placed in some sort of order with typed information between each one. There were also quite a few medals displayed. He would have liked to stay longer to read about them but, he suddenly didn't want anything to do with the place, or at least, no more than he had to. Once tonight was over, he'd probably never be in here again.

Flo and Mavis were both fed up with people asking where Beryl was. Nel, next door, seemed to be doing more washing than usual so that she could be hanging it out, hoping to see Flo. She knew there was something going on. This morning she had donkey stoned the front step twice trying to catch a word with Flo. Just as she was about to give up, Mavis came out.

"Oh! Hello, dear. You alright then? You don't seem to have been around much lately. I asked Routine Rosie if she'd seen you and she said she hadn't."

"I'm fine. I've been sorting things out indoors. Now that Beryl has moved out, there were some things we didn't need so I've been busy."

She knew that wouldn't satisfy Nel's curiosity as soon as she'd said it.

Straight away Nel said, "Where's she gone then?"

Mavis's mind was working overtime now. What could she say?

"She got fed up working at Woolworths and so she decided she'd get a job that was live-in."

Mavis was beginning to panic now. Why did she say that?

Nel looked amazed. Beryl, she thought, was still quite young to be doing something like that.

"Where's that then?"

Mavis suddenly remembered a book she'd recently read where a girl had run away from home and had got a job in a hotel on the coast.

"She's working in a hotel on the coast. The staff live in."

With her usual bluntness, Nel continued.

"Where's that then? You're all right with that? How do you know she can take care of herself?"

Mavis went to walk away but Nel had got her cornered.

"That's all a bit sudden, isn't it. I thought she was doing well at Woolworths."

Mavis had to think of something to say to end this conversation.

"They train them to do all sorts of things at those big hotels. She'll be able to learn how to do cooking and serving and, maybe, she could end up as a receptionist."

Nel crossed her arms, her ample bosom making it difficult.

"I've never stayed in a hotel. I wouldn't know what to do. I'd be scared of showing meself up. You'll have to let me know how she gets on."

Mavis was so relieved when Nel turned and went indoors. She'd been leaning against her front door and that usually meant she was going to chat for ages.

As she headed for the shops, Mavis thought, what have I done? With no real idea where Beryl was, she had created a world where she was working in a hotel. That would probably be the last place she'd be. She could only hope that she'd found a place she could safely stay and, maybe, get a job. Hopefully, it wouldn't be too long before she got in touch or even decide to come home.

Once Fred got back home, he found Annie in a bit of a state. The W.I. woman, Anthea, had heard that the family were going to have a wedding to do so she had popped around to offer her services as the wedding cake maker. She had said that their members had lots of ideas for wedding cakes and some had won prizes for them. Annie couldn't tell her the wedding was off because she didn't know what Fred had sorted out. She said she'd have to get word to her if they needed help with the cake.

Fred seemed pleased with himself. He looked around the room for the newspaper. He usually liked to have a go at the crossword when he got home from a morning shift. It helped him relax.

"Where's the paper love? I'm out later down at The British Legion Club. It's tonight. I'll have a word with Jim Venables to let him know what I've found out and that it won't be our Johnny his daughter needs to wed."

By eight o'clock, Fred had freshened up, put a shirt and tie on and got his favourite jacket out of the wardrobe to wear. Looking at himself in the full-length mirror in the bedroom, he felt ready to face Jim Venables. It wasn't going to be an easy conversation but it had to be said. He was glad he was meeting him at the club because it seemed the kind of place where order and quiet conversation was expected.

Jim was standing at the bar. He was talking to the barman. His fingers were clutched around what looked like a gin and tonic. Fred approached him. As he turned, Jim seemed surprised to see Fred, although he must have heard he'd be in to speak to him. Putting his drink down, he extended his hand. Fred shook it.

"We've got to talk. I've found out things aren't what they seemed when we last met. I think we'd better find ourselves a table."

Jim's reaction was simply to offer to get Fred a drink. Luckily, there was a corner table they could sit at. It almost seemed appropriate, Fred thought, that they'd both be in a corner. Fred accepted the beer Jim brought over.

"My Vera is driving me mad with his wedding. She's getting a suit made for it and it's costing me a fortune, what with the bride and bridesmaids' dresses. What a bloody farce. She's even telling me to arrange for the church to get the bell ringers in."

He paused and took a sip of his drink. Fred waited for him to finish. Fred decided there was no easy way to deal with this. He blurted out, "There can't be a wedding. Not to our Johnny, anyway, because the baby can't be his. He only got friendly with your Christine at her best friend's engagement party and that means she was already carrying when she met him. She must have been with someone else in the weeks before that."

Jim stared at him. The look on his face saying it all. The few seconds silence that passed seemed never ending.

"Just a minute. How do you know that for sure?"

Fred took a gulp of his beer.

"Johnny only met her that night and the timing's wrong for what your daughter told you. He'd only known her for about five weeks when she told him she was pregnant.

"The other thing is, that Irish midwife, Bridgit, told him that your Christine hadn't been to see the doc to get it all confirmed."

Jim took a gulp of his drink.

"Bloody hell! This is turning out to be a right stitch up."

The sudden realization that he'd got a lot of questions to be answered made him finish his drink in one gulp.

"I'd better get another one in. Do you want one?"

Fred felt sorry for the bloke. His little princess had deceived him.

"Let me get the drinks. You need to think what you're going to do first."

Returning with their drinks, Fred sat down feeling a lot more relieved than when he first arrived. Jim was silent.

"Can I take all this as gospel? You can see my position. I only hope the bloke that's got her pregnant is not already married."

He seemed to be taking the prospect of his daughter being easy game in a very calm way.

Fred was beginning to think this child was in a lottery before it's born.

Jim leaned back on his chair.

"You know what this means? I've got to tell Vera that Christine has been playing around and has come off the loser. She'll go mad. She's told everyone about the wedding. She's as pleased as punch that she's going to be a grandmother before her sister is. My life won't be worth living."

Although Fred had a good idea who the father was, he wasn't going to say.

"I tell you what, mate, once your girl works out who she was with a couple of months ago, you could still have a wedding on your hands."

Jim looked resigned to the fact that he was going to get home with the news and face Vera. He liked Johnny when he met him but now he was going to get to like some little randy sod he didn't know and who will probably do a runner if he's not careful. Christine wasn't the little angel he thought she was. In fact, she wasn't the daughter he knew.

CHAPTER NINE

The yard, situated in the only space available at the end of the street, was typical of an unused area, not big enough to house a building other than a small shed. The ground area had stored in it the remains of various bits of machinery left over from the war years which had been collected and dumped here. The grey concrete base of the yard had been broken up when discarded metal sections of machinery had been dropped on it. It was a pitiful sight.

The jobs that Sam had been doing to earn a living were pathetic really, when he thought about them. Collecting things that people didn't want any more now that America was sending loads of new world stuff over. Households were what people were calling 'modernizing'.

Kitchens were being transformed with gadgets and labour-saving devices. Washing boilers and mangles were being thrown away. Old tin baths were being left to rust while hanging on garden walls because bathrooms were being installed.

Shifty Sam sat alone in the yard contemplating his future. He was 35 years old. A survivor, having fought for his country, lost a lot of friends, found himself in debt and without a proper job and was looking out for his brother, Colin, who wasn't the sharpest knife in the box. There had been some problem when he was born but he never did find out what it was. Those days were when a local woman who had experienced childbirth would help. Something had obviously gone wrong. Both their parents had died a while ago and he hadn't thought to ask about Colin's problem.

Sam was a short bloke, stocky they called him and as tough as old boots. His height was no problem though and he had developed muscles while in the Army dealing with getting trucks and jeeps up and running whenever they developed faults. It was manual labour but had suited him. He was also very intelligent and had soon learnt how to drive a variety of vehicles. Once demobbed from the army, he was able to put his driving licence to good use. Getting enough money together to buy a truck, he was the 'go to' bloke if you had anything you wanted shifted.

While he was sitting in the yard, he realized this new world developing around him held opportunities for anyone who had the nous to take on the challenge. No one was going to do him any favours. He was going to have to blaze his own trail.

He'd noticed, when doing the rounds of the local streets looking for opportunities to make money, that most of the bombed houses still held a lot of old cookers, boilers, water tanks and more, all of which were rusting and useless to anyone. Even railings which had not been taken for the war effort were now standing like broken fingers stretching out to no one. They must have some value. An idea was forming in his mind. He'd heard that the government were starting to consider what to do with all this scrap metal. Their new programme of demolishing and clearing as many of these derelict properties as they could, would enable them to build new homes in this area. The sight and stigma of bombed houses was something they wanted to address.

Pre-fabricated homes were springing up for people who didn't want to leave this part of London.

The talk of new towns being created in nearby Essex was more than just rumour. Factories would be built to turn scrap iron and metal into materials for these new homes. The more he thought about it, the more it made sense for him to create his own scrap iron business. He and Colin could recover a lot of the waste household things. They could start by finding out how they could sell it to the right people. He'd have to get in touch with other scrap iron merchants to get the right contacts. Him and Colin could take the risk of getting the stuff off the bomb sites. It would be difficult but worth it. They'd got the lorry but no lifting gear.

He looked around the yard. It would be a tight fit to store the stuff but, hopefully, it wouldn't be long before anything they'd managed to pick up could be shifted.

Looking down at his hands, they were calloused and blistered with cuts and grazes that were evidence of a hard life. He would think of these scars as his apprenticeship. Now he was ready to put his experience to good use.

Sitting alone in the yard, it all seemed like a good idea, but would it be possible? He'd have to find Colin and see what he thought.

It was almost midday and he remembered there were usually quite a few local blokes in the Wagon and Horses with all sort of contacts in all kinds of trades. He might be able to find out a bit more about the scrap iron trade. He felt quite pleased with himself for coming up with this idea. He'd better get a move on or he'd miss them.

Only a few miles in distance from Shifty Sam's yard, another mental scenario was being pondered. Beryl had left the small room she was renting in a house not too far from the city. The room had been advertised by a lady whose husband had recently died.

She needed some income and was happy to share her home with lodgers. Beryl had assured the lady she was hoping to start a career working in one of the big department stores in Oxford Street and so needed accommodation near the big shops. Her reason for wanting the room seemed to satisfy the woman.

Sitting in the café with the late breakfast she had ordered, she already felt her life had changed and it hadn't frightened her. She was watching life unfolding from the window of this café. So many people. So many places they wanted to be. She was distant, and yet, she felt part of their passage into new experiences.

The early morning was bright and warm for September but by lunchtime the sky had clouded over.

She caught a reflection of herself in the café window. She looked good. As good as any other teenager who was about to apply for a job.

No one would be able to find her here. Her mum and nan never went to London's Oxford Street. They wouldn't shop here.

Having broken away from home and the people who wanted to trap her into a life that only they understood, she was of a new generation that offered more than the mundane. Today was going to be an adventure she controlled herself, or so she naively thought.

The make-up that she had chosen with Ann, which seemed so long ago now, had been carefully applied. The nail varnish used today was Poppy Red. The shop assistant had told her it was the colour everyone was using now.

Also, she had decided to wear her best silk blouse which settled gently over her young figure. The only thing she didn't want to leave behind in this bold new statement of her look was her favourite skirt. She hoped this would bring her luck.

It was time to go.

The store she had contacted was one that had opened in this regeneration of the street and was called 'Simply You'.

She had stood outside it on two occasions, staring into the huge window in awe. The milky-white form of the models arranged in the window space looked mystical with their seemingly floating silk dresses. There were also black velvet cushions arranged on a table which had glistening jewellery placed on them. They caught the light differently each time the window shopper moved.

Standing on the pavement with people dashing passed her, she could only imagine what it would be like to work in a shop like this. The people she would meet would be from a different world to the one she knew. She was lost in time and couldn't imagine anything spoiling her dream.

She was here now. Why was she still standing on the pavement outside the store?

It's now or never. She'd show her family there was life beyond the East End. It was as if trickery was drawing her in.

Once through the double glass doors she felt the first feelings of doubt in the pit of her stomach. Confronting her were an array of glass counters festooned with beautiful arrangements of whatever that department was promoting. The counters were polished and shining which made the glass seem almost invisible. She stood in the doorway, transfixed by the crystal chandeliers which lined the hallway along the store. They flashed their myriad of colours every time they detected movement below them. The area was alive with colour. It was magical.

She found herself being passed by as people were entering the store around her. Stepping forward, she was aware of a feeling of being small. Everything surrounding her seemed to have become larger than life.

Looking up, she saw a balcony encircling the entire upper floor. There were obviously wonders beyond what she could see. Was this all real? At this point, she suddenly wasn't sure if she wanted to be here at all. Had she bitten off more than she could chew? She thought back to the interview she had when she applied for a job at Woolworths. That was nerve wracking but nothing like this so far. She smiled at her memory of that. It all seemed so nothing compared to this.

She moved towards a display of chiffon scarves which had been draped across a silk screen standing nearby. She decided to stand behind them. She was hiding, and she knew it. Why was she doing that?

From out of nowhere a smartly dressed woman appeared and looked a little taken aback. She simply stared at Beryl and then put her hand up to her mouth. She looked shocked.

Beryl suddenly felt very afraid. What had she done? Why did this strange woman behave like that? This was not supposed to happen. With her thoughts in turmoil she thought she ought to turn and run. But then why should she. She hadn't done anything wrong. She then couldn't even remember which direction those double glass doors were in. The woman had turned around and run off in the direction of a room which was further away.

She decided to move forward. As she did, the aroma of nearby perfumes hit her senses. She looked around. There were people reaching out to handle the products on display. This was all new to her. With jewellery on open display, she wondered if any of it ever got stolen.

Looking across to another section, she caught a glimpse of a woman in an alcove sitting on a stool having make-up applied by an assistant. She tried not to stare at her. Was she someone famous? Should she know her from the cinema or somewhere? Maybe she was one of those models she had seen in the American magazines or something.

She was feeling herself panicking now.

This store was enormous, and she had only seen some of it. She felt so confused. She was here for an interview but she wasn't sure she wanted to be here after all.

Just then a woman carrying some boxes came towards her and stopped suddenly. She simply stared at Beryl, made a noise as though she had been startled, then turned abruptly and went back in the same direction she had come from.

This left Beryl rooted to the spot. This was all very puzzling. It was becoming unreal now. It was turning into a nightmare. Is this how people acted in these stores? Did anyone speak at all?

Stepping out from behind the scarves, she decided to find someone who could direct her to the person she had come to speak to.

At that moment, a rather tall woman walked up to her and smiled.

"Are you Miss Beryl Taylor?"

She continued to smile.

"Yes, I am. I've come for an interview for the job advertised which is for a trainee shop assistant."

What more could she say?

The woman at least hadn't run away from her. Although she did look at Beryl in a strange way.

"Perhaps you'd be good enough to follow me."

Having said that, she turned and began walking away. Beryl followed.

The store had sprung into life with customers everywhere. As she passed them, she now felt almost as if she belonged here. There was a feeling of juvenile excitement translating what she was seeing. One thing she couldn't dismiss though was the attention and reaction she saw when those other people came up to her. Had she imagined that?

The room she was taken into was an office. Why was she in an office? She wanted to work on a counter in the store. Perhaps they've got things wrong. That would explain what had happened. They thought she was someone else.

"Please sit down. I want to ask you some questions about yourself."

Beryl sat in front of the woman. She didn't know what to do next. She was feeling very vulnerable. This didn't seem like an interview. She had told them all about herself in the letter she had written to the store. What more could she tell them?

The woman leaned forward and rested her elbows on the

desk.

"My name is Mrs Carter and I'll be looking after you if you come to work for us. Can you tell me how old you are?"

"I'm sebenteen and I used to work in Woolworths."

The room went silent. She heard a door close somewhere nearby with a bang but that was all.

Mrs Carter smiled and sat back in her chair. She was thinking, this young girl had chosen to come for a job in this store when she could have chosen any of the others in the street. It was fate. This was a moment not to be lost. She must not lose her to another store, but she would have to be very careful what she said to her. At this point in time, only she knew how this scenario was panning out.

"I must apologize for the reception you were given when you came into the store. I believe a lot of people were staring at you. I'm sorry for that. You will find out later why that happened."

Beryl moved slightly in her seat. She was feeling uncomfortable and didn't know what to do or say.

Mrs Carter stood up and walked around the desk. She seemed very tall and important and Beryl was beginning to get worried, but she didn't know why. What was she going to do or say next?

Looking directly at Beryl, she said, "The man who owns this company and store lives on the top floor of this building and likes to know about the people working for him. For that reason, I would like you to come and work for us because I know he would like to meet you but there is something I have to tell you first."

Beryl was feeling even more confused. What's she

saying?

"I don't want to work in an office. I want to work in the store. Are you telling me I can have the job of counter assistant? I know I could do that."

She felt panic rising in her chest. It always happened when she was afraid of what someone was going to say to her. She must stay calm.

Mrs Carter walked back around the desk and sat down again. She leaned forward.

Beryl was thinking this was all very odd.

Mrs Carter bit on her bottom lip. Even she seemed nervous now.

"The man who will be your employer is Arnold Morris. He will be very pleased if you accepted the job with us."

Beryl still wasn't sure what was happening. Had she been given the job? They hadn't asked her many questions. What was it that this woman had said? He would like to meet me. Why? I'm sure there must be a lot of other girls who would have applied for the job.

"Now. Before I take you up to meet Mr Morris, I will take you to our coffee shop. It has only just been included in the store. It is the American influence you know. It's proving to be very popular."

Once again, Beryl wasn't sure if they understood she wanted to be in the store, not the coffee shop.

Sitting alone with the steaming cup of coffee in front of her was a good chance to watch the sales girls talking to customers, showing them the products. She was feeling a bit better now that she was on her own.

It wasn't long before Mrs Curtis came back.

"I will take you up to meet Mr Morris now. We can take the lift."

Beryl silently followed her. When the lift came to a halt, the doors opened, and they were in a corridor. As they walked along the carpet which made their steps so silent, she noticed the paintings lining the walls. They were of people from a bygone age and those people were beautifully dressed in silks and satins. There were also dark wooden chests carved with animals and patterns. On some of the chests, she could see china bowls with, what looked like dragons, on them.

At the end of this seemingly endless corridor, double doors stood partly open. They both went in. It was quiet. The room they had entered was huge. There was a window which reached from the ceiling to the floor. Beautiful curtains were hanging either side of it and she noticed embroidered tassels were holding the curtains back.

A very big desk was in the centre of the room. Behind it was a marble fireplace and over that fireplace was a large portrait. It was of a young girl. Staring at it, Beryl couldn't believe what she was seeing. It was a portrait of her! She was dumbstruck.

An elderly man was standing in the shadows at one side of the room. On seeing her, he almost seemed as dumbstruck as she was. She looked at him and he looked at her. Not a word was spoken.

At this point, Mrs Curtis stepped forward and broke the silence.

"This is Beryl Taylor, the young lady I spoke to you about."

He still didn't speak.

Beryl didn't move. The elderly man didn't move.

It seemed as if time had stood still.

Mrs Curtis moved Beryl to a nearby chair and indicated she should sit down. There was a lamp on the table next to her which showed Beryl's features clearly.

The elderly man slowly stepped forward. He stood by the desk now, simply looking at Beryl. Suddenly he came to life.

"I must apologize for my silence. Please forgive me."

As he advanced forward, Mrs Curtis moved back. She didn't say anything.

"I am sorry if I have startled you, but you look exactly like my darling granddaughter

who I lost during the war. The portrait over the fireplace could almost be you. I'm told you are seventeen years old. Pamela was the same age. She was in the wrong place when a bomb fell on the building she was in."

He stood silent for a few seconds as he stared at the portrait, silently grieving for Pamela.

Beryl had to admit the portrait could have been her. Even the girl's hair and smile were the same as hers. So that was why the people she had encountered in the store seemed almost shocked at seeing her. She understood that now.

Arnold Morris didn't want to frighten the girl. He had already, in his own mind, decided that he wanted to take her under his wing. He could encourage her to learn about the store and, maybe, she would let him guide her in the art of presentation. His beloved Pamela was just beginning to understand what he was trying to teach her about the world of business. He had hoped she would eventually become the person to take over when he could no longer cope with the management of this wonderful store.

The only sound Beryl could hear was the roar of the traffic outside. She didn't know what she was supposed to do. Sitting next to the small table, she turned to see if the silent Mrs Curtis was still there. She so wanted her to be. She was. She sensed Beryl's anxiety.

Arnold Morris broke the room's silence. Looking at Mrs Curtis he suggested she arranged some tea and cakes for them. If he could speak to Beryl casually, he might be able to get some information from her about herself – where she was from, if she was living at home with her parents, where she had worked before. He could get all this information from Mrs Curtis, of course, but he wanted Beryl to tell him all about herself. He wanted to hear her speak.

Back in Francis Road, Shifty Sam was all fired up after thinking of a way forward with his business. He wouldn't mention his plans to Colin yet. He needed to get some idea of what would be involved. He stood up and, stretching, he already felt he was on to something good here. The Wagon and Horses wasn't far and so he strode along with a purpose.

The place was packed as usual, even at this time of the day. Most of the trade's people he recognized were all in deep conversation.

Edging through the crowd, he made his way to the bar. Once he'd got a pint in his hand, he felt more like one of them.

Milling about, he could see that there were at least two blokes he knew who dealt in scrap. He made a beeline for them.

Jimmy Durrant was a big bloke. Twice the size of Shifty. He'd been in the scrap metal business since before the war. His old dad had started the firm and Jimmy had carried it on when his dad was crushed to death by some scaffolding collapsing onto him. He'd been working locally at the time and when it happened the whole street seemed to turn out to look at his crushed body. Every time it was recalled, the story became more and more gruesome. Small boys loved being told about it.

Before Shifty could approach Jimmy, he found himself herded forward into the company of a group of dust-covered labourers, none of whom he knew. Above all the general chatter he heard his name being called. He looked around. It was Jimmy. He was surprised to see Shifty in here.

With his beer slopping over the rim of the glass, he made his way over to him.

Finally getting settled, he put his ideas and questions to Jimmy who was all ears. What's more, he didn't seem too bothered about the competition from Shifty as he said there were enough damaged houses locally waiting to be stripped before the council got their hands on them. Once the push to get them demolished was on, locals wouldn't get a look in because the Government Department for Building would take over.

Shifty was beginning to think his idea would be achievable. Jimmy gave him a scribbled note where he could get rid of anything he managed to salvage. He told him to start small and see how it went. Also, there were two houses in Shifty's area which had been, more or less, flattened when a bomb meant for a nearby factory had hit the properties in the road next to it. So far as he knew, nobody had survived, and nobody had ever come by to search for any family stuff.

"That old biddy, Flo, and her nosey neighbour will probably be able to tell you who used to live there."

With all this information, Shifty finished his beer and left with more ideas going around in his head than he had arrived with.

He wanted to strike while the iron was hot. He'd go around to see Flo and get some information about those two houses. He'd seen them gradually deteriorate over the years but had never thought to see if there was anything worth salvaging. The main part of the house had come down long ago, but the basement and cellar seemed intact. He couldn't remember who'd lived there.

Flo was surprised to see Shifty at her door.

"Well, you're a sight for sore eyes. What's up?"

She could smell beer on his breath and hoped he wasn't going to cause trouble.

"Hello Flo. How you doing?"

She looked at him, not wanting to ask him in.

"I'm fine, thanks for asking. What brings you around here?"

Shifty stood with his hands thrust deep into the pockets of his old coat. He always did that as though he was trying to stay calm.

"It's some information I'm after and I think you could help me."

Flo stepped back from the door and asked him in.

The kitchen was warm. Flo had been doing some ironing on the table. She didn't like using the new ironing board they had. She still preferred to do it on a cover on the kitchen table. The wireless was playing a selection of old tunes and the whole room smelled of baking. This was very nice. It was homely.

Pointing to a chair, Flo said, “Sit yourself down and let’s get on with what you’ve come for.”

Shifty did as he was told, like a naughty schoolboy. He began asking if Flo knew who used to live in the bombed houses at the end of the street. With no hesitation, she began.

“Oh! That was Mr and Mrs Krotoski. I haven’t thought about them for years.”

She paused and put her head in her hands. She was almost saying a prayer.

Looking up, she said, “Nice people they were. It was only her and her husband living there. They came over from Poland about twenty years ago. He was in business you know, but I don’t know what. She was always well turned out and, in the winter, she used to wear a proper fur coat. We were on nodding terms but that was all. There was obviously money there.”

She paused and thought back. Nobody had ever visited the place after they died, and it seemed a bit sad.

The kitchen was suddenly silent.

“What do you want to know about them for?”

Shifty sat back on the chair. He knew he had to be careful what he told her, or his plans might get ruined.

“Oh, I was just wondering whether they had anyone go through the debris after the war. I might see if there’s anything useful left after all this time. People ask me to look out for kitchen stuff in the rubble. There’s bound to be a few things in there.”

Flo couldn’t make her mind up if he was only after a few pots and pans and, maybe, some spares for a cooker or, perhaps, taps that could be re-used or whether he thought there might be anything valuable to be discovered. Mr and Mrs Krotoski would only have bought the best of everything after all.

"Well. That's all I can tell you. I've got to get on with my ironing now."

Shifty got up and made his way to the door.

"Thanks for that. I'll see you around."

Once Flo had closed the door, she felt there was more to it than that and decided to keep a look out for Shifty, should he be seen picking over the rubble of that house. What if he found something valuable in there? Flo's interest had been stirred.

CHAPTER TEN

Shifty was surprised how confident he was feeling. His life had jogged along with no direction for too long. Seeing how things were changing, now was the time to get serious. He would speak to Colin about his plans. There wouldn't be any reason why Colin would question him and his ideas. So far, he'd taken care of him and his contribution to the new ideas would be his physical strength because he was a strong man.

As he walked along Francis Road, he became aware of how everything he was looking at had remained the same for, what seemed like, ever. He was not going to be part of this stop in time for much longer. Now, today, was going to be the start of a new beginning.

By five o'clock Mavis had returned home. She had been, once again, walking the streets, looking into shops in the hope of seeing Beryl perhaps working behind a counter somewhere. She must be earning money somewhere because the weeks had passed, and she hadn't come home.

What must she be doing? Suppose she had fallen in with what Flo called 'bad company'. What would happen if she was living in some awful room somewhere with no friends? How was she managing to get enough to eat?

Mavis could only imagine the worst.

This evening was going to be when Shifty would put his ideas to Colin. They'd go for a drink in The Bell, a pub they didn't normally use. There they could talk while having a couple of drinks without being interrupted. He'd say what was on his mind and see if Colin agreed with what he wanted to do. There'd be no reason why he wouldn't agree.

The next morning, Shifty and Colin made their first visit to the house where Mr and Mrs Krotoski used to live.

The place was in a really awful state after so long. What walls that remained were very unstable. Perhaps that's why nobody else had tried to salvage anything.

One side of the house was completely gone with an open area where one of the bedrooms used to be. The staircase consisted of a few remaining steps with the rest of it having fallen into the basement.

The steps leading down to the basement were concrete and the only thing obstructing them were some bent and twisted railings that had fallen into the shape of a cage. The old wooden basement door was still intact. It seemed that the door had never been opened since the bombing. That pleased Shifty. Maybe there would be some stuff in there they could use that wouldn't be too difficult to move.

Standing back on the pavement to get a better view, Colin noticed how the brickwork was crumbling along the remaining wall at that level. If they weren't careful, the whole thing could come down on them.

They both decided they would drive the lorry around and bring as much rope with them as they could lay their hands on. They would need to haul stuff out of there without disturbing any of those walls.

The timing was bad. Nel was coming home from the shops and she was going to pass the property. Trudging along the street, she could see Shifty's lorry parked up. She wasn't in a good mood. Her bunions were playing up. As she neared the lorry, she put her bags down. What was going on? She couldn't see anyone about. She moved to the edge of the pavement and nearer the drop into the basement. Peering down into the trashed area, she could see the old wooden door down there had been forced open because it was now splintered and in pieces. She couldn't hear anything though. Shifty and Colin must be down there somewhere. They were probably looking for anything tin, like an old bath or, maybe, some decent pots and pans. The Krotoski's always bought well.

As she couldn't see anything, she reluctantly picked up her bags and continued walking. She winced as her bunions pressed against the side of her shoes. If they got any worse, she'll have to go shopping in her slippers.

In the wreck of the basement, Colin was being very careful picking his way around, not only rotten wooden furniture that had collapsed into the basement, but also broken glass and several framed pictures that had come to rest in puddles of rainwater. Their scenes of forests and rivers which had once been vibrant had now collided with reality and made haunting pictures.

It was as if the contents of this once nice house had given up and thrown themselves away.

Shifty was on the far side of the basement where a large butler sink was still fixed on top of a cupboard, its pure white presence making it seem majestic and untouchable. Every step they took, their boots crunched onto the rubble laid before them.

Shifty was secretly having doubts of finding anything he

could salvage and pass on. They were limited to the area they found themselves in, or were they? At the far side of the basement, Shifty could see what looked like a doorway but the gloom of the basement and the trash piled over there from the collapse of the stairs made it difficult to see it properly. The rest of the property would be too dangerous to explore but they could, maybe, safely get over to that side.

Nel had arrived home. Even though she was ready to drop onto a kitchen chair with a cup of tea, she was curious about what was going on at that house. Why was Shifty's lorry there? What was he up to? Flo might know. With her fists on the table, she hauled herself up.

She'd kicked her shoes off when she sat down and now she had to find them under the table. Good job Flo was only next door.

Her front door was shut which was normal now. At one time she never closed it but, since Beryl had left, they always closed it. Almost, thought Nel, because she didn't want people asking about the absent Beryl. Closing the barn door after the horse has bolted thought Nel.

Anyway, she tapped on the glass panel in the door and waited. Mavis half opened the door as though she didn't want to see who was there. She was looking very old thought Nel.

"Hello, luv. Have you got a minute? I was hoping to speak to your mum."

Mavis opened the door fully and let her in.

Shuffling along the passage, she went into the kitchen where Flo was finishing rolling out some pastry on a board on the table. She looked up. She wasn't pleased Nel was in her kitchen. That always meant she was either spreading gossip or was after some. She straightened up and wiped her hands on her apron.

"What, do you want?"

Nel moved forward.

I saw Shifty's lorry was outside that bombed-out house down the road. What's he doing there? I would have thought that place was too dangerous to go into. There's nothing there to salvage."

She waited for an answer.

Flo drew in a deep breath and glanced over to Mavis who was standing in the doorway.

"How the hell would I know why he's there? I'm not his keeper."

Nel frowned.

"I only hope he's not sending that dopey brother of his in there to look around. He might be big and strong, but he's not all there and never has been. The poor sod could get killed."

Mavis stepped forward.

"Surely he wouldn't let him do anything silly. Why would Shifty put him in danger? No, he'll be careful."

Flo was listening to all this, knowing Nel had come on a fishing mission. She was curious enough to come asking about it all.

"You'll have to ask him about it next time you see him. I can't help you."

She picked the rolling pin up, scattered some flour over the pastry and started flattening it where she had left off but, this time, she was putting more effort into it. She was annoyed that Nel had asked about Shifty.

As the kettle obviously was not going to be put on, Nel

turned and left.

Glaring at Mavis Flo, said, “The nerve of that woman. I wouldn’t give her the satisfaction of starting a rumour, even though I know what he’s up to.”

Mavis just shook her head.

There was still plenty of daylight left and so Shifty decided to make his way over to the door he had seen. Carefully studying each bit of debris before he moved it, he was soon almost there.

The door was a sturdy one. Perhaps it led to a wine cellar or something. Those Krotoskis would probably have liked wine seeing as they were foreign. He could just make out a rusted but sturdy lock and it still had the key in it.

“Colin, come over here. We might have struck lucky. The door is locked but we will be able to get in. People only lock doors if there is something valuable behind them.”

With Colin standing next to him, he turned the rusted key and was surprised how easily it turned. Cautiously, he pushed on the door. There was something blocking it. There must be a room beyond it and something had fallen in the doorway during the bombing. He tried to peer around it but the light was not good.

“Get me a rod or something I can use to push the stuff away that’s there.”

Colin was soon back with what looked like a metal rail from the old staircase.

There was just enough room for Shifty to get his hand and part of his arm in the space so that he could dislodge what was there. Within minutes he had been able to open the door enough to see around it. There were large packing cases in there with stickers over them showing places he had only seen in books. They all looked untouched. He could also see what looked like a big, sturdy chest of drawers. Next to that was a desk or something like it. The wood was so dark that he imagined it had been soaked by the weather over the years because just above it he could see daylight.

There was also a winged armchair that had obviously once been very grand, the tapestry covering it now wet and breaking up.

Turning to Colin, the smile on his face said it all.

"I think we might be lucky here. There's bound to be some stuff in those trunks and drawers in the furniture. It's getting too dark now but if we come back in the morning good and early, we will have the whole day to get sorting."

As they drove back to the yard, Shifty was convinced there was money to be made here. The only problem they would have was to make sure they searched the basement without causing too much noise and to get whatever they salvaged into the back of the lorry and away before anyone could ask what they'd found. That would be quite a trick if they could pull it off. He would bring some tarpaulins tomorrow so that they could quickly cover their 'finds'.

The next day, Flo thought she'd call in on Annie. Now that Johnny's wedding wasn't happening, Annie had got back to herself again. It would be worth a chat with her just to catch up.

The morning was cold, and she was hoping Annie would wait a while before she went to the shops. Luckily, a lot of other neighbours seemed to think the same thing because even Routine Rosie wasn't about.

Just as she was about to knock, the door opened. Annie had been opening the curtains in the front room and saw Flo.

"I was just coming around to see you."

Annie was smiling.

"Good, because I've got some news for you. You'll never guess what's happening now? Get yourself in and I can tell you about it."

They both settled into the warm kitchen, tea cups full and biscuits out. Annie seemed, somehow, content.

"Now. When the wedding was cancelled I couldn't have been happier. That girl wasn't right for him. But, I never imagined we'd be arranging another wedding and this time one we think is right."

Flo sat perfectly still. Her cup of tea was still on the table. What was all this about?

Annie looked directly at her.

"Well, say something then."

Flo was lost for words for once.

"Who's getting married now then? Is it your daughter?"

Annie smiled.

"No, it's Johnny again but this time he has asked Niamh to marry him. They've been seeing each other for some time and it's his baby she's expecting. It's due in a couple of months. She's such a nice girl."

Flo was listening to all this, not knowing how to react. Annie had said that Niamh was such a nice girl. In Flo's eyes, she definitely wasn't that or she wouldn't have found herself pregnant. She didn't want to burst Annie's happiness bubble. She took a sip of her tea and placed it back on the table.

"Well, say something then." Annie was looking directly

at her now. She had wanted her friend to react differently.

"Well, that's a turnaround for Johnny then. Perhaps it will make him more responsible. He's always been a tearaway."

Flo helped herself to a biscuit.

"Does this mean you'll be needing me to help you with the food for a reception or are you going to have it somewhere else?"

Annie's brain was almost bursting with the ideas she had accumulated over the past few days.

"Fred is pleased because he likes Niamh. The other good thing about all this is that they can live at her grandmother's house, so that's another thing solved."

Hardly stopping to catch her breath, she continued.

"Niamh doesn't have any family other than her grandmother and so we thought we could have a nice tea in our front room for them after the wedding. With rationing ended there won't be any problem getting what we need. I can ask the neighbours in to make up the numbers. They all know Johnny and Niamh."

She stopped to take a few gulps of her tea.

"If you can help me with the tea arrangements, I'd be really grateful. We could make up a note of stuff to be bought and we could share the preparation."

Annie suddenly stood up.

"I've just had a thought. Perhaps I could get that W.I. woman, Anthea, to make us a wedding cake."

Flo was still sitting at the table. She was beginning to wonder why she was here. Annie was so animated, it had been difficult to get a word in.

"Just stop for a minute, will you."

Flo was beginning to wonder if Annie would run out of breath.

"Of course, I'll help you. When do they intend to marry and where will it be?"

Annie suddenly looked startled.

"Oh! I hadn't thought of that."

Flo stood up. She'd had enough.

"I'm pleased for you, girl, and hope things go better this time. I've got to go now but let me know when you've got things sorted. It won't be long before the whole street knows and so you're going to have a lot of questions to answer every time you go out."

Strolling back home, Flo's thoughts turned to Beryl. She wondered where she was and what she was doing. How was she managing? She hoped that her story would have a good ending. Little did she know how good Beryl's story would end. The lifestyle ahead of her would be beyond Flo and Mavis's imagination. Life was full of chances and unexpected turns and Beryl's life was going to change as one door closed and another opened.

Shifty and Colin had arrived at the bombed house early. It was a bright morning and it hadn't rained last night. They were soon at the partly opened wooden door. It had been anything metal they were after when they first got here but, who knows what they'd find now. Shifty had spent most of the night tossing and turning but he didn't feel tired. He was feeling lucky.

Carefully easing himself through the open space, Colin followed, wondering why Shifty had decided this was a job worth doing. Everything that was lying around was ruined anyway. What could possibly be here for them?

Shifty made his way over to the desk. The drawers had remained shut during the bombardment, but the brass handles were now in a sorry state. One of them was hanging away from the woodwork. He tugged on one of the other handles. The drawer was stiff, but it finally opened. The papers in there included the passports of Mr and Mrs Krotoski. Their photographs showed them looking very stern. He turned some of the pages. They were stamped with visits to Italy and America.

Placing them on the top of the desk, he pulled out another of the drawers. This one contained a journal detailing financial transactions with letters from an auction house based in London. It was obvious that quite a lot of antiques had been purchased over the pre-war years. Where were they now, he wondered? He added the journal to the pile of papers.

A drawer in the centre of the desk would not budge. The desk was badly damaged already and so he had no qualms about forcing it open with the screwdriver he'd brought with him. It gave way with a creak and split at the front of it.

Easing it open, he found two small leather pouches. His heart began to beat a little faster.

Colin looked surprised at how good the condition of the leather was. It had been well protected.

Shifty opened the first pouch and tipped its contents onto the top of the desk. A small velvet purse appeared. Opening it up, Shifty could see what looked like a brooch. He carefully drew it out. It was beautiful. It was a flamingo. The body of it was glistening with what could be diamonds. Its head was shaped with other coloured stones and the legs of the bird were a gold colour. Could this be valuable? Surely it must be what, in his mind, he called 'the real thing'.

He looked at Colin and they were both speechless.

The second pouch contained a gentleman's gold watch. It was completely undamaged, its face as porcelain white as the day it had been made.

Shifty drew in a deep breath. Looking at Colin, he said, "What we've got here could be worth a tidy sum. We'll have to get that bloke with the jewellery shop in the high street to have a look at them."

Colin looked a bit worried.

"Suppose he thinks we nicked them. He might call the police."

Shifty wasn't bothered about that. He was going through the other drawers in the desk but didn't find anything in them worth bothering about.

The chest of drawers only had clothes in it and they all gave off the smell of mould.

Next, he would see if he could get the packing cases open.

They tried to pull them across the rough floor to get a better look at them but whatever was inside seemed to weigh them down.

They both fell back against the wall, causing a shower of brick dust to fall. They looked up. The ceiling still seemed intact.

"We'll have to find something to force them open."

Searching around, they found a rusty crowbar and wedged it against the lock. With a crack, the lock split and the top of the first case was free to open.

All they could see were newspapers. Masses of them.

Pushing them aside, they saw the first glint of silver. They had discovered a lot of elaborate candlesticks.

Shifty looked at Colin.

"We could be on to a winner here."

He sat back away from the trunk.

"You remember that bloke we sold them medals to that we found the other week? You know, the ones that bloke was interested in. We could get in touch with him about a lot of this. He don't ask any questions."

Colin seemed worried. He looked across the room and noticed a wooden crucifix on the far wall. Even after the bombing and all the damage to the house, that crucifix stayed on the wall. He swallowed hard.

"We're robbing the dead."

"Don't be bloody daft. Nobody has come to go through this stuff. We know the Krotoski's didn't have any family. Are you telling me that if and when the council get around to demolishing this place, they're going to chuck this stuff away?"

Colin stayed silent.

By the end of the day, they'd managed to haul everything they wanted out of the cellar and into the back of the lorry. A tarpaulin had been put over everything before any questions could be asked. If they wanted to make any money out of this lot, they'd have to start contacting the right people who were on the wrong side of the law. Shifty knew they'd have no trouble earning from this little episode.

Francis Road seemed to have settled down a bit now. There were no rumours doing the rounds about neighbours. Most of them were looking forward to the wedding of Johnny and Niamh and then the birth of the baby. Fred and Annie seemed to be in better spirits as well. There hadn't been much to celebrate recently but now the party for the bride and groom would bring everyone together. The only person still missing from all this was Beryl. She had been gone for some weeks now.

Arnold Morris had spent a lot of time with Beryl and together with the help of Mrs Carter, they had coaxed out of her most of her background. They had persuaded her

to leave the small room she had been renting and had given her a room of her own above the store. She would be trained in all aspects of the business, just as Pamela would have been. She was beginning to feel very special. She had also been able to choose a whole new load of clothes and had been accepted by the staff she had been introduced to.

Arnold Morris had become a changed man since Beryl arrived. He had confided in Mrs Carter that fate had brought his beloved granddaughter back to him. She knew it was the strange and uncanny resemblance Beryl and Pamela had. This young girl's future was set.

Grace felt as though a weight had been lifted from her since she had met the elderly gentleman in the café. She had to do something soon to get away from London. She needed a new beginning. She knew when Tom and Martine would be away from the flat and so planned the best time to collect her things. She wouldn't leave them a note. She would simply leave her key on the table.

Wondering where to go, she remembered Justin had a colourful poster of a beach somewhere in Cornwall enlarged for the studio to use as a backdrop for girls modelling swimming costumes. It had stayed in her memory because she didn't know anywhere could be so beautiful.

That was it. With her few belongings packed into one small case, it dawned on her how pathetic that was. Striding out, she made her way to Paddington Station, bought a one-way ticket to Newquay and decided that could be a starting point for her new life.

As she clambered aboard the train, she looked at her ticket. The number of the booked seat was 48. This was a corridor train and it seemed to go on forever. Finally, she found her seat in a carriage that was occupied by an elderly couple. She hoped they wouldn't want to strike up a conversation because this was going to be a long journey. She settled back into her seat, the unfamiliar but pleasant smell of the train in her nostrils. As the train pulled out of the station, she closed her eyes as if she didn't want to see London any more. She had no reason to look back.

Grace alighted from the train at Newquay. She had bought a tourist map for Cornwall from the station kiosk and after she had studied it she thought she would make her way along the coast to Perranporth. It had been a sudden decision made from desperation.

She wanted to get as far away as she could and had decided that Cornwall was the place to go. She booked into a small family hotel and knew she had enough savings to last about three weeks. She would have to find work as soon as possible. What could she do? What was she capable of? It had been so long since she'd had to make any decisions. She was feeling a bit pathetic.

Walking along the coastal path one morning, she stopped

and gazed out across the ocean. It seemed endless, disappearing into the horizon. Seagulls were noisily swooping above her. They seemed so big.

She thought back to the defining time she had spent in the library.

With the wind blowing her hair across her face, she was trying to convince herself she wasn't hiding but seeking a new life. It had only been a few weeks since she had made the decision to leave her past life behind and that was what she had done.

Making her way down to the beach, she could see the vast beauty of it. The tide had only recently ebbed away and left it pristine. How, she thought, could something as violent as the sea, leave the sand so flawless.

As she looked to the far end of the beach, she could see a crowd of people. There were some trucks there as well. Trying to focus, she could also see what looked like some equipment and part of the beach had been roped off. She stood with her hand shielding her eyes from the sun to see better.

She didn't want this to be some awful incident where, perhaps, someone had drowned. That would be horrible. Why else would there be all the activity that was going on? Although she didn't really want to know, she felt compelled to see what was happening.

As she approached the group, she could hear laughing. Then she stopped dead in her tracks. There was some camera equipment there. Emerging from the crowd, a small man carrying a clipboard approached her. He was smiling.

"Sorry if we have taken up a bit of your beach. We're shooting a scene about an orphan girl who has run away from home but has been found by some boys in one of their beach hideaways. We've tried doing the scene loads of ways but still can't get it right. We might be some time. We had to wait for the water to recede."

Grace didn't know what to say.

"You can stay and watch if you like. Are you local?"

"No. I'm from London and only arrived a few days ago. It's a new start for me. Next thing is finding a job."

"Well, I'm Dave and this motley crew are the cast of my film. Only amateur, you know. We're new and you're new and so why don't you meet us in the pub tonight for a drink. We don't bite."

Having said that, he turned and went back to the job in hand.

How extraordinary.

Grace took her shoes off and created footsteps in the sand as she slowly walked back along the beach. It was sad. They would be gone in a few hours and she would be forgotten. She had, however, already made her mind up that she would meet with them all at the pub in town – The Lobster Pot. This was going to be interesting.

It was almost 8.30 when she arrived, and the film crew were already there. As soon as she could, she found a gap at the bar. She was feeling like a fish out of water. She smiled to herself. That was appropriate.

Within minutes, she had been spotted and quite literally pulled over to the lively group taking up a long table which was already strewn with half-empty glasses. The conversation flowed easily and noisily.

By the time the evening had almost ended, she had been

introduced to all the group but could not remember their names. They had enthusiastically told her about the theatrical company they had formed, and they were, so far, making some money touring with it all over the country.

One of the group, Michael, introduced himself as the script writer. He was about 25 and said he was originally from London. Taking Grace away from the throng, he obviously wanted to talk.

"So, what did you do before you ran away to sea?" He was smiling.

She liked his sense of humour.

"I was a make-up girl for a modelling agency."

She knew this was not completely true, but he wouldn't know that, and it was close to the truth.

"I would try to make the models look good in front of the camera."

There! She had labelled herself.

"And you decided you wanted more from life?"

She looked down. She didn't want to look directly at him. What was he going to coax out of her next?

"Yes. You could say the people I worked with were not the people I wanted to work with. It was just a job."

"Before you tell me more, let me get you a drink."

By the time he returned, Grace had already decided she wanted to know more about him. It had been a long time since she had felt so relaxed in male company.

"In the business I am in, we find people come and go, not staying with us for very long. It's the travelling you see. As soon as one project has been completed, we need a new location."

He took a sip from his drink.

"You told Dave that you had just arrived in Perranporth. I didn't think I'd seen you before. I would have remembered. I hear you are looking for work."

He paused but Grace didn't say anything.

"You wouldn't like to join us as a make-up girl, would you? We would pay you. If you don't mind being on the move all the time it would help us out and, if you say you want to work with people you could get on with, why not give us a try?"

She didn't know what to say. This offer had come as a great surprise. Was she ready to make such a commitment? She didn't want to jump out of the frying pan into the fire.

The silence worried Michael.

"Do you need to think about it? The offer will still be there in the morning."

He laughed at the expression on her face. Was it shock or horror?

Nothing more was said that evening but by the time they had all decided to take to their beds, Grace knew she had found the freedom she had been looking for. Yes, she would join this happy band of players. She also knew that Michael was the reason.

CHAPTER ELEVEN

It was now just over two years since Beryl had made her escape through that scullery window. Mavis had kept in contact with Ann, who had been Beryl's best friend. She hadn't heard from her either.

Francis Road had settled into its own routine existence. Johnny and Niamh had got married in a very lively and public ceremony with just about everyone from the area attending just to make sure it was properly celebrated. Fred and Annie were very pleased how all the neighbours had joined in with supplying the food and drink. It was a proper East End reception. When eventually little Joe arrived, he was loved to bits by everyone. He was now two years old.

Sadly, One-leg Len had died. He had gone out for his usual lunchtime drink but hadn't returned home. Edna was getting worried. He'd not been himself lately.

With the help of a couple of his old drinking pals, they had retraced his usual route back. They found him. He was sitting on the War Memorial steps, propped up against the granite column. There were two empty brown ale bottles to one side of him. He was obviously dead, his head hanging forward. He had died with a couple of his WW1 medals in his pocket and, clutched in his hand, was a yellowing creased photograph of men in a trench, and one of them was Len. Oddly, he had taken his shoe off and it had fallen onto the pavement. It was as if he had made his mind up that he wasn't going to take another step.

His wife, Edna, couldn't afford to hire the church hall and so Flo and Nel had arranged with the vicar to have a couple of trestle tables put up in the church garden and the neighbours would contribute some sandwiches and cakes. The publican at the end of the street contributed a crate of beer and a bottle of sherry for the occasion.

Edna drew the front room curtains when he died, and she never opened them again.

His funeral was delayed by a couple of weeks because the street didn't want it to clash anywhere near little Joe's birthday.

Routine Rosie had finally stopped going out and now needed a lot of help with shopping and taking care of herself. She had taken to sitting in her open doorway with her feet outside on the small step there. Any and all passers were greeted by her and felt obliged to stop and chat.

Shifty Sam and Colin had found people to buy the stuff they had retrieved from the Krotoski house with no questions asked and had set up their new scrap business in a decent yard a couple of miles away. They were doing OK.

The rest of Fred and Annie's children were no trouble to them. Sarah, who had remained living in Kent, had reached 21 and so the family who had taken her in during the war were throwing a special party for her which Fred and Annie and the other boys were at. They were very proud of her. She was what people called 'a woman with prospects who was going places' although Fred and Annie didn't understand what that meant.

Nel, Flo's busybody neighbour kept asking why Flo and

Mavis hadn't treated themselves to a few days away during the summer to visit Beryl on the coast. She thought there was more to the story that Beryl was supposedly working in a hotel somewhere on the coast. They hadn't said which coast.

Mavis hadn't given up hope of finding Beryl. She just wanted her home.

George was doing well at the bakers and was now apprenticed and learning all the things about cake making. His artistic talents were showing themselves as he progressed onto decorating wedding, anniversary and birthday cakes. He was now getting orders from caterers and hotels.

In the two birthdays since Beryl had left, Mavis quietly wondered if George would ever get the opportunity to bake and decorate a cake for her.

Mavis decided this morning she would have to go up to Woolworths because there were several things she'd run out of in the kitchen. She'd used Woolworths less and less since the incident when Elaine Davenport had come around with those photos. She was still feeling embarrassed about it all.

"I'm going up to Woolworths this morning, Mum. Is there anything you want while I'm out?"

Flo was in and out of the scullery transferring the washed clothes from the boiler to the mangle and then onto the line in the garden. She looked up at the sky. It didn't look too heavy and, maybe, most of this washing would get dry before any rain came. She was hoping Shifty could find her one of the washing machines he'd told her about but, so far, one hadn't appeared.

She hated taking stuff to the bag wash. Sometimes you ended up with an article of clothing that belonged to the previous user. That wasn't nice.

"No. I don't need anything."

Mavis decided she wouldn't catch the bus this morning. She'd stroll up the high street to the shops. Passing Benny's Café on the way, she heard her name being called out. It was Joan, Ann's mum, tea towel in hand.

"Have you got a minute?"

Reluctantly, Mavis made her way over to Joan.

"I'm glad I've seen you. I've got a bit of good news to tell you."

The smile on her face couldn't have been broader.

Mavis's heart skipped a beat. Was she going to say that Beryl had been in touch with Ann? Please let that be the news.

They went into the café.

"Sit yourself down and I'll get us a cuppa."

A minute or two passed and Mavis could hardly stop herself demanding the news.

Finally, Joan sat down with the teas.

"You'll never guess. My Ann is getting engaged. She's been with Peter for over a year now and they've decided to get married in a few months. Ann will be 19 in a month's time."

Joan continued.

"She's asked me to ask you if you'd come with us to choose a wedding dress. She wants to go up to Oxford Street and look around some of their shops for one. She'll never find anything nice local."

Mavis felt trapped and dashed at the news. It wasn't what she had hoped for. She would have to say she'd go with them.

Once arrangements had been made, she continued her walk up to Woolworths.

The shop was busy as usual. She often met people in there that she'd known for years. What would they all do without Woolworths? The one person she didn't want to meet was Elaine Davenport.

Once she'd got what she came for, she made her way home. She just kept thinking about Joan's news. She was happy for her and it was nice that Ann wanted her to be part of the search for a dress. Would she ever get the chance to do the same with Beryl?

Back home, she told Flo the news, who didn't really understand why Mavis had been roped into the dress search.

"That'll cost her a bit. They know how to charge up there."

Sitting in the smart office of the Simply You department store, Beryl was pouring over ledgers and payment slips. Arnold had asked his accountants to teach her the

rudiments of accounting and she quite liked the fact she could follow through the process of buying the stock, displaying and selling it and finally being able to balance the books. She had always been good at maths and found the whole process very satisfying.

She had also been taken under the wing of the buyer for the Ladies Boutique. Her choices of the latest fashions were, very much the same, as Beryl's.

Arnold had ensured that the range of expensive make-up and perfumes they stocked were brought to her attention as well.

She would soon be 19 and felt the luckiest person in the world that Arnold had taken her into his life and given her all these opportunities. What would she be doing if she hadn't made her escape that night?

She sat back into the leather swivel chair at her desk. Taking a moment to let her mind wander, she recalled how Arnold had taken her for tea at The Ritz, which she had heard about, lunch at a place called Simpsons in the Strand that she had never heard of and on a special evening event when she accompanied him, she found herself in a beautiful restaurant with glistening chandeliers and carpets she could sink into at The Savoy Hotel.

She had learned about fine dining.

She could have been in wonderland for all she knew but, in reality, she was still only a few miles from where her previous life had begun.

Coming out of the thoughts clouding the day's routine, she found it was time she visited the various departments in the store to see if all was running smoothly. Arnold had asked her to engage and speak with the staff. It was important she got their trust and opinions.

She had become a beautiful and confident young woman; her auburn hair now rested on her shoulders and had a glow which shone out with every movement.

She was slim and had acquired a sophistication she wasn't aware of.

She rarely thought of her life in Francis Road and had no regrets at leaving that all behind. Should she feel guilty? Had she worried her mum and nan half to death?

When Arnold had first taken her into his care, she didn't know what direction her life would go in but had grown confident enough to trust his teachings. She silently acknowledged family birthdays when they came around but, had decided she wouldn't contact anyone about them. That might lead to the slippery slope taking her away from the wonderful life she was now enjoying.

Wandering around the store, she found it easy to chat to whoever wanted her attention. Everyone had accepted her as part of their retail family. Life couldn't get any better.

This morning Joan was as excited as a child at Christmas. Her Ann was soon going to be married to a very nice young man with job prospects better than they had hoped.

Ann had made it quite clear that she didn't want a wedding dress made by a local woman. She wanted to buy one from a London department store. Neither Joan or Mavis had been in a department store.

It was nice to be going somewhere special.

Flo, in her wisdom, told the three of them to guard their cash in case they got pick pocketed. She heard there were a lot of people up there who were always looking for people like them, far too trusting.

The day arrived and none of them could have imagined its outcome.

Mavis found Joan and Ann waiting for her. They both looked very nice with Joan wearing a suit that had been bought for someone else's wedding and Ann looking very grown up in a tunic and blouse that, apparently, was the fashion now. She had lost touch with the latest fashion trends since Beryl left.

"Mrs Taylor, would you mind if I called you Mavis while we're shopping? It doesn't seem right if I keep calling you Mrs Taylor."

Mavis smiled.

“Yes, of course you can.”

As they set off, they didn’t really have a plan. They had no idea how many shops would be in Oxford Street but there must be at least one that sold wedding dresses.

There was no way Joan was going up to Oxford Street on an underground train. The thought of being stuck in a tunnel frightened the life out of her. She’d been on the ghost train at the fair and nearly passed out in the darkness. She persuaded the others that they should go by bus. She felt more in control on a bus.

At the end of the unfamiliar journey, they finally got off the bus and were immediately shocked at how many people were milling about. Joan was feeling a bit confused already.

“Surely not all these people are shopping for clothes.”

Mavis smiled.

“All these stores sell more than clothes. They sell just about everything. That’s why they’re called department stores. They have lots of different departments.”

Ann’s eyes were darting everywhere as she observed, not only the shop windows and their beautiful displays, but everyone around her.

Joan already seemed to be dragging behind a bit as they entered their third store.

Once inside, Ann stopped dead. She was looking around trying not to miss anything. The polished counters in front of her seemed to hold more glittering treasures than she could ever have imagined. Customers were being encouraged to handle the items they wanted to buy. This was all so new to her.

“Look, Mavis, I can see some lifts.”

She was pointing to a wall of marble and metal doorways.

"I've never been in a lift. Let's go upstairs and see what's there."

She was striding across the floor at a pace. She stopped.

"Look, Mum. They even have a list of what you can buy upstairs."

She was pointing to the lay-out of the departments.

Joan was not sure if they needed permission to go into the lift and up to the next floor. This was a very posh shop. Oh, she was so out of her depth.

Smiling, she said, "Well, how about that. It says ladies clothing and wedding dresses are on the first floor and so we'd better go up there."

Mavis found herself being in charge as Joan was looking more and more bewildered.

Guiding them into the lift, they were on their way up.

The first floor did have wonderful wedding dresses but, on inspection, they were all far too expensive for Ann. She was very disappointed. Her savings would not go far for one of those.

Joan needed a break.

"Let's get out of here and find somewhere we can have a cup of tea. Perhaps after that we might find a store with what you are looking for,"

They all agreed and made their way back onto the street.

Ann was almost in tears.

"I didn't know it would be this difficult to find a dress."

They had been in stores that were very grand and had prices to match. They had been in stores where all the assistants seemed far too important to help them and they had been in stores where even the customers were better dressed than they were. What Flo would call 'All fur coat and no knickers'.

Joan paid for the teas and they all decided they would go into a couple more stores before they gave up their search.

It was afternoon now and just ahead of them were two stores Ann recognized the names of. One was the famous Selfridges and the other was Simply You. That one had been mentioned in one of her favourite magazines.

Reaching Selfridges, they all stood in awe, looking at the wonderful window displays.

Mavis simply uttered, "Now, that's what I call style."

She was awestruck at the sight of the beautiful clothes draped over a row of lifelike models, the spotlights making them seem almost real. So clever she thought.

They moved along the pavement to look at another huge window. It was magical. This one was displaying lots of velvet cushions which had beautiful jewellery placed on them. With the backdrop behind them being black, Mavis was astonished at how brilliant the gemstones shone.

This store was obviously living up to its reputation.

They didn't have time to look at any more windows. Ann was getting impatient. She wanted to get in there. Mavis wondered if there was anything here they could afford. Joan just didn't understand what she was seeing.

As they approached the huge door, a uniformed doorman held it open for them. They looked around them. It was for no one else. He smiled.

It wasn't long before they all decided this place wasn't for them. At least they could say they had been inside Selfridges.

With a sigh, they all wearily made their way to Simply You. If they couldn't find what they were looking for here, they would return home.

Once through the double glass doors, they all stood silently looking down the avenue in front of them. Joan was staring at a beautifully created tiered display of chocolates that looked too good to eat. The smell of the chocolate was overpowering. She was in love. She felt revived.

Mavis walked forward towards a stand which drew her to the unmistakable smell of leather. Stacked high were highly polished cases and trunks which could hold lots of secrets once they were locked.

Ann had been drawn to an area where perfume was being sprayed from an atomizer. There seemed to be people trying to choose a fragrance that suited them.

Everything they were silently observing seemed unreal.

Breaking the silence, Joan looked at Mavis and said, "Do you think they sell wedding dresses here? We ought to ask. This is going to be our last shop."

"They must do. We'll probably have to go up to the next floor where they have clothes."

Ann was looking very despondent. These shops were grander and more expensive than she could have imagined. She was beginning to think this had been a wasted journey.

Mavis could see how disappointed Ann was getting.

"Let's go up to the next floor and have a look around anyway."

Ann looked over at her mum.

"OK. love. As this is our last store, let's see if they've got anything you can afford."

This lift had an attendant who called out what could be found on this floor.

Back in the office, Beryl looked out of the huge window overlooking the street. She was now used to the scene in front of her. So many people looking for something special. Where had they all come from?

Simply You was more than just another department store on this famous street. It was, she hoped, welcoming.

This was one of the few moments she allowed herself to dwell on the past. She wondered if she would ever have found a path to this store without the good luck which brought her here. Arnold was taking her training to another level of responsibility. She could choose a department to promote.

As she observed the melee in the street below, she started to think what would he do? He would consider what time of the year it was. It was springtime and lots of girls would want a June wedding. They were probably, even now, thinking about wedding dresses, flowers, printed invitations and all the other things that made a wedding special.

Standing alone in the office, she spoke out aloud, "I will promote summer brides with our wonderful collection of wedding dresses."

She was so pleased with her idea, she felt she must check on their stock straight away and have a word with the staff in that department. There was a good team there. They wanted their customers to be pleased with the help and advice they were given.

As she entered the staff lift taking her down to the floor below, it would deliver her to a small room behind the department area. She felt this was going to be a good day.

She'd made an executive decision. She would tell Arnold all about it later.

Ann was first out of the lift with a weary Joan and Mavis following. What they saw were rails and rails of wedding dresses. A feeling of panic enveloped her. She looked at her mother.

"What are we doing here? I've made a mistake. I should never have thought that someone like me could have enough money saved up to buy a dress from here."

Mavis stepped forward. She'd decided that even if they wouldn't be buying one of these dresses, they would at least have a look at one or two and Ann should try one on. She wondered how well they were made.

There were other people looking at them as well. These people, she decided, were genuine buyers. They ran their fingers along the crystals which were expertly sewn into the bodices of the dresses.

An assistant stepped forward.

"Would you like to see one of the dresses taken off the rail?"

In the meantime, before she went into the department, Beryl decided to observe what was happening out there. Arnold had always told her to watch people and see how they reacted to the products. Opening the door only a fraction, she could see people milling about at each of the counters. Some girls were trying on tiny tiaras with trailing lace falling over their shoulders. Another young woman emerged from a changing room wearing one of their most popular dresses. The tiers of silk falling gently to the floor. She stood in front of a large mirror and she looked wonderful. A range of velvet slippers in pastel shades with silver buckles were finding lots of buyers.

She then cast her eyes to where a sales girl was taking a dress from the rail and showing it to another customer. Beryl gasped. The customer was her friend Ann. Standing not too far from her, Beryl saw Joan and her own mother. How could that be? Why was Ann looking at wedding dresses? Why was her own mother in the store with her as well as Joan? They never came to Oxford Street to shop.

It was all too much. She burst into tears and sobbed silently into a handkerchief. She must find Arnold. She wanted to tell him what she had just witnessed. Ann would never be able to buy one of their dresses. She knew she couldn't face her own mother in this state. She must speak to him.

Arnold was in his sitting room at the top of the building not knowing what was about to happen. Beryl burst into the room in floods of tears. Arnold put his newspaper down and stood up. What was going on?

Beryl literally threw herself at him. He pulled her in and held her tightly. He'd never seen her like this before.

After calming her down he suggested they sit down so that he could find out what had happened.

Beryl still wasn't over the shock of seeing her mother and the others in the store. This had been her hiding place and the new life she had made here. What was happening? There were so many questions she wanted to ask. She burst into tears again.

Arnold decided he wouldn't be able to make any sense out of all this. He decided he'd go down to the department and just observe these people. Why was Beryl so determined not to approach them? She hadn't told him one of the customers was her mother.

As he walked among the customers, he was drawn to a group of three women. They seemed out of place. Although they were looking at the dresses, they were very hesitant. They almost didn't want to touch them. He decided he would approach them. The sales girl hadn't made any progress with them. She wasn't sure what to do.

"Good afternoon ladies. May I introduce myself. I am Arnold Morris and this is my store. I hope you find what you're looking for."

He was trying to sound casual.

The sales girl smiled. She was thankful for some help here. Mavis was first to speak.

"We were all admiring these beautiful dresses. A bride would love to be seen in any one of them."

Pointing to a silent and shocked Joan, she said, "My friend's daughter will be getting married this summer and we all thought we would help in the search for the perfect dress."

Being the salesman that he was, Arnold smiled. "I'm sure this young lady would make a beautiful bride."

Joan and Ann still hadn't said a word.

Trying to keep his conversation going, he looked at Mavis.

"Do you have any daughters?"

Without hesitation, Mavis said, "Yes. I have a daughter who will be 19 very soon. She lives away from home."

Why was she talking to a stranger about Beryl?

"Well, I hope when she decides to get married, she finds her perfect dress here. Just like your friend's daughter."

Mavis sighed.

"I don't think Beryl would be able to buy one of these dresses. They all cost a bit more than she could save."

Arnold held his breath for a few seconds. She said her daughter's name was Beryl. She said she was not living at home. He could also detect Mavis was from the East End. Had Beryl caught a glimpse of her mother in the Store? That might explain the tears. She hadn't felt ready to speak to her. He mustn't lose this opportunity to find out more.

Turning his attention to Joan.

"Perhaps if your daughter can find a dress she likes, as the store is running a Special Event, I would like to give her the dress and, with your permission, we could take a photograph of her wearing it for our window display."

The sales girl couldn't believe what she was hearing. There was no Special Event. Joan, Mavis and Ann couldn't believe what they were hearing. Their shocked expressions said it all.

Arnold was doing what he did best. Solving a problem and promoting the store. His sudden decision to take this step was typical of him.

"Perhaps your daughter would like to choose a dress and then we can make any alterations to it before it is delivered to her."

His intention was that Beryl would be the one to take the dress to the customer and, perhaps, reunite with her family. Her home would continue to be with him at the store. He did not want to lose her.

They couldn't believe what they were hearing.

Joan suddenly found her voice. "Can you do that?"

He smiled. "I can do anything I want to. This is my store."

After convincing them the offer was genuine, the sales girl helped Ann choose the dress she wanted and then took her into a small side room to pin the alterations required.

Arnold in the meantime, went up to his apartment where he had left Beryl, hoping his news would calm her down. She agreed to be the one to deliver the dress providing she could use Arnold's own car and his driver would wait until she was ready to come back home to the store.

CHAPTER TWELVE

Mavis, Joan and Ann couldn't get back home quick enough. They had all been unusually quiet on the bus taking them home. They were all still in shock.

Joan and Ann went home in a very confused state. Was that all real? What had just happened?

They had both decided that if they didn't hear from the store in the next couple of weeks, they would just put it down to a peculiar experience. They couldn't tell anyone about it because no one would believe them. The one thing they did arrange though was to say they wanted the finished dress to be delivered to 4 Francis Road where Mavis lived. Joan couldn't have it delivered to the café.

If it did turn up, it would be a miracle. If it didn't, Ann would still have time to find one herself. She decided to tell Peter what had happened. He thought the whole thing was laughable.

When Flo heard the key in the front door, she was half asleep in the armchair. The cup of tea she'd poured herself was still in the cup but was now cold. She pulled herself up.

Looking at the clock, she couldn't believe the time. Mavis had been out all day.

Mavis looked exhausted. She almost threw herself at the kitchen chair.

"I'll put the kettle on now that you're back. What's taken

so long?

She shuffled into the scullery and filled the kettle. Looking for the matches to light the gas under the kettle, she glanced over to where Mavis was sitting. She hadn't moved since she came in.

Flo took a cup down from the shelf and put it in front of her.

"Are you all right? You haven't said a word."

Mavis drew in a deep breath.

Looking at Flo, she said, "You'll never guess what happened today. Not in a million years."

Pouring the tea, Flo was waiting to hear.

"Well, I won't know if you don't tell me, will I."

Mavis didn't seem interested in the tea. She didn't know where to start.

Flo was getting impatient now.

"Well, did she get a frock or not? She hasn't spent more than she can afford has she?"

She continued with a look of concern on her face. She blurted out, "You didn't get robbed, did you?"

At last, Mavis came to life.

"We went to loads of shops up there, but everything was much too expensive. We almost gave up. You can't imagine some of the things we saw. It's another world."

Flo was now sitting at the table.

"Get on with it then."

Mavis smiled.

"No, we didn't get robbed and yes Ann did get a frock. She got one that is so beautiful she will look like a princess when she gets married. It has been beautifully made and has some small beads embroidered into the bodice. There's yards of material in it. When she tried it on, she looked as though she was floating."

Flo frowned.

"I bet that needed a huge box to get it home. How did you manage on the bus? It sounds as though it would need a seat to itself."

She chuckled.

"Did you have to buy it a ticket?"

Mavis visibly relaxed a bit.

"We didn't bring it home with us. The store is making some necessary alterations to it to make sure it is perfect. They are going to let Ann know when it will be delivered. She's arranging for it to be brought here. Joan didn't want it delivered to the cafe."

There, she had said it.

Flo straightened up.

"What shop did she buy it in? How much did it cost? If it's as good as you say, how could she afford it? I hope you didn't lend her any money."

Mavis took a sip of tea.

"It didn't cost her anything. The store gave it to her as they were having what they call a Special Event. We even met the bloke who owns the store. It's called Simply You."

"What! You've been taken for a ride there. No one gives a wedding dress away for nothing, especially if it's a good one. You mark my words, they'll be a surprise at the end of the day. They'll probably give Ann another dress. One that hasn't sold well, and she might find they'll give her a bill for delivering it."

All this was what she expected her mum to say. She hoped she wasn't right.

Joan and Ann were still reeling from the day. Once they heard from Simply You, they'd all meet up at Mavis's house.

Beryl had calmed down by the evening. She and Arnold had decided they would have a quiet meal in his apartment. His beloved Beryl had been so upset. He decided to ask her outright if one of the women he spoke to was, in fact, her mother.

"Did you get upset because your mother was in the store? If that was the case, I can understand how shocked you were. Please tell me you will take the dress to your friend when it's ready. The address for the delivery is 4 Francis Road. Is that where your friend lives?"

Beryl was beginning to feel panic rising again. This would mean she would have to go back from where she had escaped. Arnold knew very little of her background. She had kept that a secret.

"Yes, my mother was the one you were speaking to. The address for the delivery is where I used to live. I don't know if I can go back there."

Arnold didn't want to miss the opportunity to make things right for Beryl. The delivery would only need to be a fleeting visit, but that could lead to, perhaps, a time when Beryl would feel able to see her mother more often.

He looked directly at her.

"Once the dress is ready, you might be more used to the idea. There's no reason why you can't be in touch with your family. You know you will always belong here."

The next few days seemed to speed by and Beryl didn't

want them to. She was still afraid she wouldn't be able to go back to Francis Road.

Finally, the dress was ready. It was placed in a large white box along with oceans of tissue paper. The box was sealed, and a wide ribbon was wrapped around it.

"Do you want me to write to your friend to let her know the dress is ready? She will have to be there when it's delivered."

He was trying to sound as casual as he could.

Arnold was looking directly at Beryl. He wanted her to make the final decision.

Beryl drew in a deep breath. She mustn't put it off any longer. It was, after all, only a visit.

"Yes. Let's do it."

Right up until the last minute, Beryl wasn't feeling very sure about this. Arnold's driver was at the front of the store. The boxed dress had been put in the boot of the car. Beryl had changed her outfit three times and had brushed her shoulder length hair until it bounced. She stood in front of the mirror and decided it was time to leave.

As the car drew away from the store, Beryl pushed herself hard back into the seat. It was almost as if she was trying to slow the car down. The traffic was slowing the car down without her help.

As the journey continued, she averted her eyes. She didn't want to see what she had left behind.

Nobody knew who was delivering the dress. She knew her best friend Ann would be waiting for it, together with her own mother. Also, of course, her gran would be all eyes to see the dress which had, no doubt, been described and talked about for the last couple of weeks. Flo was still expecting there would be disappointment. The deal she had been told about couldn't be true. She'd never heard anything like it.

As the car found its way among the East End streets, Beryl finally looked out of the window. Nothing had changed. There were still bomb-damaged houses on some of the streets and corner shops with boxes of food stacked up in front of them. The sky was grey, and the light seemed to take all the colour from what she was seeing.

Her thoughts returned to Oxford Street and all the colours that seemed to create dreams in her mind. The lights from the shop windows were like diamonds dancing on a lake. Those images could never be extinguished.

Finally, they arrived.

To have a grand car draw up in Francis Road would cause a stir. To have it stop at Number 4 would be something to observe. Curtains would be twitching.

The driver parked directly outside No. 4. He took the box from the boot and opened

the car door for Beryl to get out. She hesitated. He handed the box to her. She left the safety of the car and got out and stood with the box clutched to her chest so that her face would be hidden. She knew her gran would be in the front room looking out for the car. She also knew that she would be looking out to see who else was watching.

It was just a few steps to the front door. Before she had a chance to raise the familiar knocker, the door opened. Mavis stood in the doorway. Beryl lowered the box to reveal her face.

Mavis visibly gasped. She put her hand to her mouth as though stifling a scream.

"Hello, Mum."

Beryl was rooted to the spot. She didn't move and neither did Mavis. There they both silently stood. Time had stopped. They both seemed to be holding their breath.

A noise from the passage was Ann excitedly coming to collect the box. Flo had called out that it had arrived. As Ann approached the door, she looked past Mavis and saw Beryl. In her own mind she recognized her, but she looked somehow different. She didn't know what to do. Finally, she turned and went back into the kitchen.

Mavis finally smiled and moved back so that Beryl could get into the passage. She stepped forward.

Beryl was immediately aware of the familiar smell of cooking. She looked to one side and saw the hooks on the wall were, as usual, struggling to stop the coats from falling to the floor. She looked up. The same lightshade with the crack in it was still

hanging at a slight angle.

Putting the box down, Beryl grabbed her mother and tried to stop herself crying. It didn't work.

Mavis wrapped her arms around Beryl and stood like a sentry guarding a treasure.

Wondering what was going on, Flo and Ann both appeared in the kitchen doorway. On seeing Beryl, Flo cried out, "Christ Almighty, where did you come from?"

The next few moments were a mixture of disbelief, wonder and shock.

They all finally found their way into the kitchen. Mavis put the box on the table. Joan was still silent but watching what was happening. She was also staring at Beryl. She looked so sophisticated. She was beautiful. She had the look of a model. Her make-up and the suit she was wearing made her look like a stranger to Francis Road and the East End street she was now in.

Minutes had passed in total confusion. Ann finally stepped forward.

Would you all let me see my dress. I need to unpack it."

She wasn't annoyed that Beryl had seemed to have stolen the moment of its arrival but, she was getting annoyed that everyone seemed to be ignoring her and it was because of her that they were all here.

With everyone still in shock, the small kitchen was suddenly a scene of frantic turmoil. Joan still couldn't stop staring at Beryl. Why has she been the person to deliver the dress? What connection did she have with that store? Did she work at Simply You? They didn't see her when they were there. That store was in London. Mavis had told everyone she was working in a hotel on the coast. Why had she said that?

With the ribbon of the box, tissue paper was flying across the table. The dress lay there with the beaded bodice the first thing to be seen. Ann gently lifted it up. It was as wonderful as she remembered. They all gathered around in stunned silence.

With a click of a key in the lock and the familiar shout, George had arrived home from work. Before he even reached the kitchen, he called out, "There's a limousine parked outside with some bloke sitting in it. Have we won the Pools or something?"

Another two strides and he had reached the kitchen. On seeing Beryl, he stopped dead in his tracks.

"Bloody hell."

The time had come to bring some order to things.

Mavis stepped forward.

"Ann, why don't you and your mum go into the front room and put the dress on. We'd all like to see you wearing it."

Beryl was standing by the scullery door. George was staring at her.

"Where have you been? All my mates think you must have got pregnant and run away. Did you get pregnant?"

Flo and Mavis were waiting for her to answer.

"No. I didn't get pregnant."

She was feeling trapped. She remembered that feeling.

Suddenly, in the doorway, Ann appeared looking like the perfect bride. She was all smiles.

Time was running away. Beryl was losing her hard-earned composure. She suddenly blurted out, "There's so much to tell you. I live and work at the store where you bought the dress. The man that spoke to you has taken me under his wing. He is training and teaching me how to run the store when he gets too old to do it. Please don't be cross with me, but I have to leave now. Please tell me you'll agree to come up to the store if I arrange for the car to pick you up. It will take some time to explain everything."

Before she could say any more, there was a knock on the front door.

"Who the hell is that now?"

Flo was very annoyed.

"It's not your driver is it?"

Pulling the front door open, Nel was standing there.

"Well, it looks like you've hit the jackpot. What's going on?"

Flo wasn't going to fall into the trap of explaining things while Nel was on the doorstep.

"One of Beryl's friends bought a wedding dress from a posh shop in London and it has just been delivered here instead of her mum's café. That driver bloke brought it and one of the people from the shop came to give it to her. We are just making sure it fits all right."

That sounded a final explanation and Flo wasn't going to go into anything else about things.

Pushing the door to close it, Flo wondered if she'd got away with it. No. She hadn't.

Nel had a habit of being just close enough to the door surround that meant her face would prevent Flo from shutting it.

"Well, can I see the frock? I know quality when I see it and if you say it's from a posh shop, I bet it's nice."

Flo had had enough.

"No, you can't see it and it's time that driver got back to the shop."

With a determined push, she finally managed to close the door.

Beryl had said her goodbyes and exchanged hugs with everyone, except George, who didn't want his sister hugging him. At least he could tell his mates about Beryl now he'd spoken to her.

As she got into the car, she noticed quite a few net curtains along the terrace had been pulled aside which, of course, meant that her mum would have quite a few questions to answer.

During the journey home, Beryl liked that thought, 'journey home' she had left them all with a visit to arrange and a wedding to organize.

She sat silently in the back of the car. She felt released and yet restrained. That goodbye was just a glance. She felt that when something was wrong, she had finally made it right.

It was now two years since Tom and Martine found themselves working with vulnerable young girls who seemed very willing to co-operate with their set-up. The photos were getting more explicit and the customers were paying any price to get their hands on them. Business was good.

They had wondered what had made Grace suddenly leave but, they didn't really care. Friendships in their business came and went.

Martine had decided that they should renew their stock of clothes at the salon. Tom agreed and told her she could go 'up West' to replenish their scanty lingerie. His customers were becoming more hopeful of being able to dwell on the sight of not just a hint of the untouched areas of these innocent girls, but full photos of them partly hidden behind fine lace which exposed and satisfied his customers' needs. There could be no harm in that. The girls were safe as long they as they no contact with his customers.

Martine decided she would visit some of the best shops along Oxford Street because it was quality she wanted. Tom didn't take an interest in what the girls wore for the photo shoots, but Martine had been aware for some time now that the finest lingerie aroused more than just visual pleasure. It made the basic instincts a step closer for their customers.

The day was bright, and Martine decided she would leave early and go up West on the underground. It would deliver her just where she wanted to be.

As usual, the street was crowded with people trying to reach their own destinations. She could hear so many foreign accents. It was as if she was shopping in a foreign country. She was feeling excited about being here.

As she walked along, she wondered what it would be like to work in one of these stores. They were vast, almost like palaces with all their splendour. Their window displays reminded her of the glamour of some of the films she had seen at the cinema. She felt a bit intimidated when going into some of these stores.

She decided to look around in some of the smaller shops. She could feel her confidence returning.

By midday, she hadn't seen anything she wanted to buy. Time for a break she thought.

Walking along the crowded pavement, dodging the people who almost seemed to be deliberately stopping her progress, she found a café where she decided she would stop for a tea and some cake.

The place was almost full, with just one table vacant. She placed her order and sat down. It was next to a large window where she observed the frantic efforts of so many people trying to find their way to unknown destinations.

For no reason at all, her thoughts turned to Grace. She wondered where she was now. Had she made a better life for herself? She hoped so. Grace had been a good friend.

The clutter of the cups and plates and the noise of the various conversations going on around her, broke her train of thought. It was time to continue with her search for the new lingerie. She renewed her lipstick and, looking into her small handbag mirror, she felt she looked as good as any of those heavily made-up shop assistants she had seen. In fact, she felt she looked good.

Stepping outside, the warmth of the sun on her face made her look skywards. The clouds had gone from the sky and the doubts she had before now also seemed to have gone.

Feeling more positive, she decided to head for one of the big stores at the other end of Oxford Street. Surely, they would have what she was looking for. Simply You would be her target.

Arnold Morris was pleased with the way he had dealt with Beryl's problem. She was proving to be a good listener and a fast learner. She was going to be good for the store in the future which had developed quite a reputation for quality products.

With the store now filling up with customers, the large double glass doors at the entrance had been left open.

When Martine finally reached Simply You, she stood inside, seemingly surrounded by treasures. The displays in front of her took her breath away. She remained still observing it all. Her senses couldn't take it in. She had found paradise.

Customers were walking in front of her and around her. She felt rooted to the ground.

Directly in front of her were the double doors of a lift. They parted. Coming out from the lift was a tall slim woman who was impeccably dressed, her auburn hair bouncing on her shoulders. What was it about that, that made her stare at the woman? As she walked confidently across the patterned tiled floor, her stiletto heels clicking, there seemed to be something familiar to Martine about her. She needed to think. She obviously wasn't a customer. She must work here.

The woman continued walking on and, on her route, she kept stopping to talk to the assistants behind the glass counters. Martine thought she had the confidence that only came from wealth and position in society. How lucky she was. Did she know how lucky?

Martine finally found her way to the department she needed. Her search had paid off. She found exactly what she had been looking for. Tom would be impressed with her choice but probably not the amount of money she had spent.

Moving between some of the other departments, even with all their distractions, Martine couldn't rid herself of the fact that woman seemed familiar. But how could she be?

Tightly clutching the handles of the bag which contained her precious purchases, she felt special that she had shopped here. She wandered on, almost not wanting to leave.

Among the sounds surrounding her, she heard the name 'Beryl' being called out. She turned. There was that woman again but this time she had been called over to one of the counters. She silently observed her.

Could she be the Beryl she knew? Surely not. How could it be? What was she doing here? She would approach her.

Waiting for the right moment and waiting for her nerves to calm down, she slowly walked over to where the woman was. Sensing someone behind her, she turned. Both Martine and Beryl were locked in a knowing silence. Neither moved.

"It is you, isn't it?"

Martine had found her voice.

"I thought I recognized you even though you've changed

a lot."

Quite calmly, Beryl said, "Hello, Martine. It's good to see you after so long."

A silence fell on them. It was as if they were the only people in the vicinity even though they were surrounded by shoppers. They seemed on an island on their own.

Looking at the bag Martine was clutching, she said, "I hope you've been able to buy the things you wanted. We have some wonderful things here."

Martine smiled a knowing smile. Beryl had said 'We'. She seemed to have got herself into a nice job here.

"Yes, I found what I wanted and more. It's a nice store. Perhaps we'll meet again."

She turned abruptly and left.

As Martine joined the throng of people, all on their own grand tour, amid the noise and clamour, her mind was trying was trying to make sense of what had just happened. Beryl had changed a lot, although no matter what, no influences she had discovered, she was still the girl from the East End who had posed for Tom. Perhaps she had forgotten that.

The train ride home felt never ending. Wait until she told Tom about Beryl's good fortune.

In the store, Beryl suddenly felt trapped for no reason at all. It was as if that chance meeting had locked her into a cage of memories. She had never told Arnold about Tom, Justin and those photos. She would not mention to Arnold that part of her life unless she really had to.

Tom was nowhere to be seen when Martine reached the flat. How cheap and nasty it looked as she entered it. The world she had just left behind only a few miles away could have been only in her imagination, but it wasn't.

She put the bag down and walked over to the window. The sun was still dodging the clouds and its reflection coming into the flat only drew her attention to the miserable state the place was in. Since Grace had left, it all seemed so neglected. She wanted to leave but she had nowhere to go. How sad was that, she thought?

Before today, her world had been a series of tasks and targets to get the girls they needed for Justin's salon. Tom had made a good living out of selling those photos but what had she achieved? Grace had left and was probably very happy with her new life, whatever that was, because she hadn't returned. Beryl had followed her own pathway and had obviously taken the right road. It occurred to Martine that they had both taken chances. Who knows what was out there.

She slumped down onto the old and worn settee. She couldn't get the aroma of those wonderful perfumes out of her mind. She wouldn't be able to forget the sheer luxury of feeling the silk lingerie she had chosen.

Opening the bag at her feet, she carefully removed the tissue paper nestling around the lace and ribbons on the lingerie. She didn't want to disturb the way the items had fallen together, almost seeking protection from what they had been bought for.

She kicked her shoes off. She was feeling defiant. Her initial thrill of having the news that Beryl seemed now settled into a lifestyle beyond anything that could have been imagined, made an intense feeling of jealousy overwhelm her. The few words she and Beryl had said in the store, now seemed to deliberately cut short any chance of finding out more.

In the silence of the flat, she suddenly heard the clank of the lift being drawn up and knew Tom would be coming in at any moment. She was now in a bad mood. She sat waiting to hear the key in the lock.

As soon as he saw her, he knew something was wrong.

"Did you get the stuff you wanted? I bet you were spoilt for choice up there. I see you've got a bag there. Show me what you got."

He walked over to the small bar in the corner of the room and poured himself a drink.

"I've had a good day. Those latest snaps Justin took of that blonde girl came out a treat. She certainly wasn't shy."

Martine remained silent.

Looking at her, he said, "Well, say something then."

Martine straightened up.

"You'll never guess who I bumped into today. Not in a million years."

She then fell silent again.

Tom was now gulping his drink and waiting for Martine to say more.

"All right then. Tell me. I'm not playing a bloody guessing game."

"Beryl!"

"Never. Where did you see her? Did you get to speak to her?"

Martine stood up and walked over to the window. It was as if she didn't want to face him when telling him her news.

"She's got herself a nice life now. She seems to be part of the management team in that big store Simply You. She's changed a lot now and swans around talking to customers and staff as she pleases."

"What!" Tom couldn't believe what he was hearing. His mind was already racing.

"If she's got a decent job, that would mean she's on a decent wage. She'll want to keep her reputation intact if she's friendly with those posh customers."

He sat down with a thud. He was smiling. "Who'd guess she'd make good."

The smile was still on his face.

"I'm going over to the salon. Justin will still have those old photos of her. Perhaps they could come in useful. I could visit her at the store to see if she wants to buy them. Simply You, wasn't it?"

Martine suddenly felt afraid. She didn't know why. Was he talking about blackmail? Surely not. That sort of thing usually ends up in the hands of the police. No. He can't mean that. She'd be drawn into it as well. Her mind was in a panic of thoughts. He was out of the door in a flash, leaving her feeling sick.

The next day he was feeling good and looking very smart in a suit that had cost him a few bob, as he had put it, but it made him open for compliments.

He took a chance at being able to see Beryl, who he was sure he'd still recognize, just by turning up at Simply You. If she had got herself hooked up with management, they'd be very interested in the snaps he'd got of her.

Sitting on the Underground train, he tapped his inside jacket pocket as though making sure his precious cargo was safe.

The store was impressive. Everything about it was, in his

mind, sheer quality. He was feeling confident.

He made his way over to the first male assistant he could see.

"Excuse me. Do you have a Beryl Taylor working here? I'm an old friend and hoped to see her while I'm in London."

The man peered over Tom's shoulder.

"Yes, we do. You've just missed her. She was talking to some customers. I could phone the office to see if she's available. What's your name?"

Tom realized that as soon as his name was mentioned, Beryl would know that Martine had told him about their meeting. She might refuse to see him.

"No. Don't bother her. I'll see her another time."

He then made his way to the entrance and stood out of sight from the assistant. He would keep an eye out for Beryl. She'd probably show up some time.

An hour had passed. Still no sign of Beryl. He would try another tactic, one that would get him some attention. He would leave a message for her to get in touch with him. He left the store.

The Guardsman, a pub in the street behind Simply You would be a good place to go so that he could write a note to Beryl. He'd have to buy a notepad and envelopes first. This note would have to be delivered in a sealed envelope, marked Private and Confidential.

With a gin and tonic in front of him, he began writing. The message wasn't threatening. It simply reminded her that he still had the original photos she had willingly posed for at the salon. Would she like to purchase them now that her circumstances had changed? She should contact him for a meeting.

There. That wasn't an unreasonable request was it?

With the envelope delivered to the store, Tom returned home.

Beryl was in her office that afternoon, feeling satisfied at the way she had sorted out a minor problem with one of the orders for delivery of material.

The envelope arrived at her desk. It was handwritten. That was unusual.

Reaching into the desk drawer, she took out the letter opener and slit it along the top of the envelope. The folded paper inside was, perhaps, from a satisfied customer. She opened it up.

As soon as she saw the telephone number written on the top of the note, she didn't want to read its contents. Immediately, her surprise at seeing Martine in the store flashed back to her. Please no, she thought, don't let them ruin her new life. What would Arnold think? Where would she get the money to buy the photos back? How much would she have to pay? She was shaking.

Arnold must never know about this. She would find a way to deal with it.

The rest of the day passed as though she was in a nightmare that she couldn't wake up from.

She would make an excuse for not wanting to have dinner with Arnold tonight. That would give her time to come to terms with the situation. She wasn't a very good actress and Arnold guessed there was something wrong.

She insisted there was nothing she needed to tell him. Finally, the dam burst, and she collapsed onto the couch next to her. He immediately put his arms around her shaking body until the crying stopped. His beloved Pamela would always cry like that when something had upset her. The memories came back to haunt him at that moment.

During the next hour, Beryl had poured her heart out to him. She felt she had deceived him by not telling him about her past. She showed him the note. His expression didn't change when reading it. He put the letter down. He poured himself a whisky.

Looking at Beryl sitting crumpled and in despair on the couch, he simply said, "I knew all about your past when you came into my life. Before I decided to nurture you, like any tried and tested businessman, I had your background checked. You must understand that I had to make sure you were the naïve girl that came, by chance, into my focus. You mean everything to me. During the last two years I have not been happier. Thank you for that.

"This letter will be passed to my solicitors and dealt with. This man will not be troubling you again. To try to extort money from you for some innocent photos is tantamount to blackmail and, I can assure you, he will be out of your life for good.

"Tomorrow, I will instruct my solicitors to take the necessary steps to end this."

Why did she ever doubt her protector would fail her? She couldn't help wondering what Tom's reaction would be to all this. For the first time today, she smiled.

Martine was wondering what the reaction would be when Tom told her about the hand-delivered note. She hoped he would get his comeuppance.

Grace had escaped, and Beryl had escaped. Maybe, now, she thought, it was time she turned her life around.

The next day, she took a chance and left.